MW01634299

Broken Arrow
Press

Advance Praise for
The Unredeemed

"D. László Conhaim's novel *The Unredeemed* depicts in vivid detail how children, taken by Apaches, adapted to tribal life and considered their captors to be family. What truly sets this story apart is its focus on the perseverance of their original kin in recovering them. I highly recommend *The Unredeemed*. It's captivating."

—Lucia St. Clair Robson,
bestselling author of *Ride the Wind*

"[A] notable approach that differentiates *The Unredeemed* from the typical Western is its attention to diversity. African Americans are prominently represented here in the Old West … a Western that excels in its sense of place, and whose unusual mix of characters makes it hard to put down and satisfyingly unpredictable. *The Unredeemed* should join *Comanche Captive* in any collection [of] Western novels and Native American history."

—*Midwest Book Review*

"Conhaim is a strong writer who brings both the desert setting and the battle scenes to life with economic but evocative phrasing … The novel makes a solid attempt to bring the Black experience into a traditional Western, and it largely succeeds … While players from *Comanche Captive* appear in the book, mainly in cameo roles, the sequel stands alone, and new readers will have no trouble following the plot … A well-written Western [that] takes a multilayered look at the past."

—*Kirkus Reviews*

Praise for D. László Conhaim's
Comanche Captive

"With *Comanche Captive*, D. László Conhaim makes the unusual choice of telling the story of a woman's resolute quest after she is taken from the band of Indians who had captured her. With drama, humor, and vivid detail, he creates an unflinching view of the harsh complexities of life on the frontier."

—Lucia St. Clair Robson,
bestselling author of *Ride the Wind*

"A deftly crafted and simply riveting read from cover to cover … very highly recommended."
—*Midwest Book Review*

"Conhaim offsets this brutal tale of human cruelty, injustice, and violence with rich descriptions of the natural beauty of the West. Recommended."
—*Library Journal*

"*Comanche Captive*'s rich characterizations bring a fascinating period of American history to life … page turning … thought provoking."
—Michael Belfiore,
author of *The Department of Mad Scientists*

"A resolute woman teams up with a retired soldier in this Western set in post–Civil War Texas … Conhaim is a cinematic writer, and his descriptions are captivating … [he] displays substantial knowledge of the tribes he writes about and creates Native American characters who are as fully developed as his white players. An engrossing tale of the Old West."
—*Kirkus Reviews*

Praise for
All Man's Land

Finalist Best Traditional Novel
2020 Western Writers of America
Spur Awards

"Maverick" Winner
2020 Will Rogers
Medallion Awards

"Conhaim draws on various elements of the classic Western … to tell a story inspired by his longtime fascination with the singer and activist Paul Robeson … Benjamin is a compelling, multilayered protagonist who moves beyond his Robeson inspiration … The prose is vivid and often dramatic, which makes for a memorable read … A well-developed and thoughtful novel of right and wrong in the Old West."
—*Kirkus Reviews*

"Inspired by the music and life of Paul Robeson, D. László Conhaim's *All Man's Land* … reminds the reader that the most unlikely of relationships can form even in spaces where they should not exist … Seeing the humanity in another person is a meaningful sub-theme … We are battling, still, with many of the themes addressed in this book … I thoroughly enjoyed [it] … It is a book that should be read in classrooms and community book clubs. It is one to add to the discussion of race relations as this country should be *All Man's Land.*"
—Christian Starr,
ThyBlackMan.com

"D. László Conhaim pens a sequel to *Comanche Captive* in the form of a tribute novella to Paul Robeson: *All Man's Land*. Robeson, an African-American bass baritone concert artist and actor, was recognized for his musical performances and cultural accomplishments, but his political activism made him a controversial figure admired by some and reviled by others. Set in turn-of-the-century Wyoming, *All Man's Land* personifies Robeson in the character Benjamin Neill—Civil War hero, a learned man, a masterful singer, a political progressive, a man of the people and a prophet—who comes to town to settle a score. Conhaim packs gunfights, villains, intrigue, mystery, plot twists, some romance and a happy ending into this vivid, entertaining read."
—Michael Searles, *Roundup Magazine*,
Western Writers of America

"Conhaim transfers [Paul Robeson's] story to the American West and incarnates Robeson in the fictitious Benjamin Neill, son of a slave, and a war veteran whose talent and courage parallel Robeson's. Conhaim's prose is spare but potent and the pages turn in the blink of an eye. I couldn't help but be reminded of the great TV show "Deadwood" for the authenticity of his supporting players, but at its heart it is a story about freedom and values."
—Terrance Gelenter, *The Paris Insider Readers Circle*

THE UNREDEEMED

A novel

D. László Conhaim

THE UNREDEEMED

Broken Arrow Press, 2566 West Lake of the Isles Pkwy,
Minneapolis, MN 55405, USA

Inquiries to Tom Mayer: tom@brokenarrowpress.com

Cover and interior design by Velin@Perseus-Design.com
Cover photo (Death Valley Dune) © Terry Thompson
www.TerryThompsonPhoto.com
Cover design contributor:
Nicole Nodland www.nicolenodland.com
Author photo: Bridget Mayer
Logo by Michael R. Geffen

First paperback edition published December 2021

ISBN 978-0-9843175-3-0

Visit the author's website: dlaszloconhaim.com

For my daughter, Shir

Author's Note

Any accounting of settlers abducted by the tribes of the Southwest—or "Indian captives," to use the common term— leads quickly to the remarkable tale of Herman Lehmann. In his 1927 autobiography, *Nine Years Among the Indians*, Lehmann recounts how he and his fellow warriors raided white settlements and camps "to get more horses, and to kill as many of the palefaces as we could." In fact, so complete is his "Indianization"[1] that when a deadly altercation causes him to flee his adoptive Apache tribe, his destination is not his previous home in Mason, Texas. Instead he lays low on the southern plains before seeking out and joining a Comanche band. Later, Herman Lehmann is among the last Comanche holdouts to surrender to the Fort Sill reservation, and there he lives until his eventual discovery and return to a mother he no longer recognizes, and who no longer recognizes him.

---

[1] By contrast, the Federal government had its own policy of "Americanization" of reservation Indians—or in today's parlance "cultural genocide": a system by which the conquered and resettled tribes were schooled in farming, ranching, English, and—yes—Christianity.

Although this work draws from Lehmann's story, its departures are many, not least of which is a young man's unspoken reason for remaining in his adoptive world. But this is also the first fictional retelling in decades of The Buffalo Soldier Tragedy of 1877, which makes it a triracial story.

To those today who would question the legitimacy of a white author populating his story with Native American and African-American characters, the author asks how else could the multiracial struggle for the American West be told except through inclusiveness? Until such time that novels of racial diversity are written by committee, this author will continue to write about other peoples too.

Finally, the use of period language herein is employed in the interests of realism.

"This was life! Ah, how he loved it! Civilization held nothing like this in its narrow and circumscribed sphere, hemmed in by restrictions and conventionalities."

—Edgar Rice Burroughs' Tarzan on his return to Africa

Prologue

Since breakfast, Gunter Hermann's two boys had been scarecrowing up and down the rows of corn, belting out nursery rhymes in their native tongue. To swallow and sparrow alike, the present song, "I'm Happy About My Goat," was as terrifying as any other. A northerly breeze carried their sweet voices afar, reaching Gunter behind his ox-drawn hand plow at the edge of the property. Here, the pests had already ravaged the crop and today's toils anticipated tomorrow's replanting. His boys always delighted in doing the corn-jobbing too. In fact, with their buoyant singsong in his ears, Gunter was just picturing thirteen-year-old Karl and younger Freddie hunched over their hand planters—stop, squeeze, start—stop, squeeze, start—when over his left shoulder a clap of wings split the air.

He craned his neck toward the creekside cottonwoods as a mass of avian specks burst skyward. This occurrence might have satisfied him, but it was unlikely that his boys' far-off singing provoked this particular flurry. Gunter pressed down on the plow handles, halting the ox. He drew a dusty sleeve across his brow and scanned the area. Could it be Indians?

Loyal Valley had been spared raids in recent months, indeed there'd even been some trade between settlers and natives. Gunter let his breath out. It was probably nothing—like so many other false alarms to the wary pioneer. But the boys should be warned nevertheless, thought this veteran of the Second Schleswig War. Gunter didn't trust peace. His cautious gaze followed the line of cottonwoods southward toward Karl and Freddie's presumed location in the fields, but the lodgepole house soon obstructed his view. His wife, Trude, seemed to share his concern, for she was on the porch, peering into the morning's amber glow and now urgently calling the boys' names.

Heedlessly, the brothers went on singing.

Gunter was already on the move toward the house, and seconds later he vaulted onto the deck by the corner rail. This time Trude didn't berate him for tracking soil, didn't even notice his dirty boots. Now another feathered flight broke aloft from the crops behind him. Whirling about, he registered this disturbance as markedly closer. Too close. With a turn of his chin, he ordered Trude to bring his rifle.

"Mein Gott," she gasped before vanishing into the house to comply.

He leaned into the H-frame at the top of the stairs, trying to follow the singing back to its source, his grip tightening. Again at his side, Trude, with blanched skin and determined eyes, thrust the weapon forward in both hands. But what good was it really? He couldn't blindly target the patch with the boys somewhere in there. Gunter and his wife exchanged worried looks as he jacked the lever. He stepped away and fired three warning shots.

The singing ceased.

Part I
The Women

Chapter One

Concealed in some scrub brush on a gentle, grassy rise above the firelit camp, black sergeant Emanuel "Tops" Chance cursed under his breath and gritted his teeth. About fifty feet away, Karl and little Freddie Hermann sat with their backs to a raging campfire, bound at the wrists. Before them towered an especially grand tepee wrapped in three bands of color, each bearing its own set of illustrations difficult at dusk to make out. It was surely the headman's lodge. Above the hills beyond, daylight was draining into the horizon like a wash of blood.

Behind Chance on the opposite side of the knoll, his men were dismounting, praying their chargers would stay quiet, while settling in at his side was Scott Renald, an ex-army captain and today a civilian scout. Renald had lost his wife and unborn child in an Indian raid. His blue eyes narrowed as he whispered, "There they are …"

A few warriors began kicking dirt in the boys' faces. After a hard flight with their bounty, they were up for some fun in the form of initiations. Little Freddie remained hunched over, as if his cinched hands held a great weight—that is, until a pop from the fire sent him jolting forward. *"Mutter! Mutter!"* he cried.

By failing this ritual test of a prisoner's mettle, sobbing Freddie was risking death or trade to another band or tribe. Next to him, older and bigger Karl cursed their tormentors in German.

This was the principal Northern People camp of the Lipan Apache—a sprawling, itinerant village on Texas' sparsely-settled share of the Chihuahuan Desert. In all there might be thirty lodges here in tepees and brushwood wikiups. Throughout, the returned raiders were sorting loot and reuniting with their families. One young warrior, his attention roused by Freddie's whimpers, tried prodding him in the eye with the nock of an arrow. Twisting away, Freddie got it in the ear instead. He burst into fresh sobs.

"Why d'ya think they took a pair of boys this time?" Chance asked Renald, crouched beside him.

The seasoned captive hunter answered matter-of-factly. "Low birthrate, short lives. German is good stock. The older one looks prime." Renald shot Chance a look. "Now what?"

That was the question on everybody's mind. Before they'd broken off to follow the trail, Captain Norton, bivouacked with the main column back at the Pecos River, ordered Chance to report before engaging the enemy. From this location a galloper needed about half an hour to exchange communications. Meantime the light was failing while those braves were thinking up new ways to haze their captives.

Pondering Renald's question, Chance smoothed his thin mustache. "I been mulling that over. Can't move the company in by stealth …"

"Yep, too risky."

"But I gotta follow orders, Mr. Renald."

"*You* do," Renald acknowledged. "But I don't. I'm not Army anymore, Tops." He pointed toward those boys. "Just look at that …"

A young but man-grown Apache was now towering over the Hermann brothers with his legs apart, extinguishing Karl's belligerence in a stream of urine.

"Poor kid," said Chance.

"Just how much longer must we delay, Tops?"

First Sergeant Chance held up a gloved signal finger. "We ought not," he replied.

Sergeant Tyler promptly crawled in behind him. Chance hesitated beside the white point man who reported directly to Captain Norton. He'd expected the black Corporal Miller to respond to his summons. Uncomfortable giving an order to a white man, he said only, "See that down there?"

Tyler understood, volunteering, "I'll inform Captain Norton." He slipped away without saluting.

Below, a second warrior with a full bladder replaced the first whose bladder was spent. Dropping his cloth skirt and setting his feet apart, the thick-shouldered brave continued Karl's humiliation. This brought the tall and clean-shaven Renald to his feet. "Well, *I* sure as hell ain't waiting for any orders." He unfastened his gunsling and let it fall, a sign he intended to enter the camp—peaceably?

"Mr. Renald!" Chance protested, but the army searcher had already started downhill.

However justified Renald's decision was, it would have deadly consequences for both sides—not just today, but again three years hence.

Chance watched with mouth agape as the villagers began noticing the newcomer with cries of, "White man!" The assaulting warrior, still holding his member in both hands, turned, trickling, in Renald's direction. Across from the boys—and behind the brave—the tepee door abruptly flapped open, and out stepped an elder adjusting his headdress. As the warrior hiked up his skirt, the headman caught sight of the white intruder. Renald, moving fast with his gloved hands open at his sides, approached the miserable pair of boys. He acknowledged them with a nod before hauling off a blow that laid their assailant flat on his back.

"Shit!" Chance cursed. He rose from the brush, clutching Renald's gunbelt. "Mount up!"

Corporal Miller was crouched just steps away. He met Tops in a standing position.

"You say their pony herd is penned to the south?" Chance asked.

"Yessir!"

"Well then, take a couple men and stampede it!"

* * *

Back in camp, the warrior's fellow tribesmen fanned out behind him, raising their weapons—but the chief lifted a hand to restrain them. Perhaps due to the fighter's youth, the elder decided he should prove himself without assistance.

Responding to his cue, the fighter sprang from his back onto his moccasins, pulling his dagger, but Renald was ready with a "feint and blow." He struck the brave in the face a second time. Stunned, his opponent dropped the blade and reeled back with a shattered nose. Renald took the fight to him with a barrage of fists, and the line of tribesmen broke to make way. Finally, Renald sent the youth stumbling backward over a looted crate marked "Flour." Not even this setback ended the Apache warrior's determination to vanquish his white foe. He bounded onto the box, using it as a springboard to propel himself against Renald, who, absorbing the impact on his shoulders and moving with the weight, caught the fighting man's neck in one hand, his thigh in the other, and then heaved him into the fire.

This was too much for the Lipan men. As their champion rolled out of the flames, singed and shrieking, they started for Renald with war whoops. Fortunately for the paleface, the troop's bugle sounded and at once Chance and all his mounted men came crashing down into the encampment.

Their skyward gunfire and battle cries were met by more whoops and yelps. Bullets whizzed and arrows whooshed, and in the melée Renald was driven face first into the ground by a dagger-wielding assailant. It could've been his end, but his attacker immediately took a bullet to the brain. From his horse, Chance—his revolver smoking—tossed Renald his gunsling, then got bumped away by another charger struggling for footing. Gunfire crackled around them. Ducking, Renald sought visual confirmation that the brothers were all right. He found them bowed with their backs to the licking flames as more lead and arrows sliced the air. For now, the boys were quite alone, their captors occupied instead with saving themselves and their families.

A raging fire had started somewhere in the camp. Feeling the smoke in his throat, Renald had just seconds to act before he would certainly be attacked again. What could he accomplish in this chaos? Should he go for the boys or go for the chief? A rescue attempt would draw fire and further endanger the boys. But taking possession of the headman could cause the Indians to surrender. It would be easier too. Nobody was protecting the chief as he stood outside his tepee, his jaw locked and his eyes dark and mournful.

Like a boulder slide, the troops thunderously rolled through the camp, destroying everything and discharging their weapons. But not without mishaps. A charger went down, pinning its trooper and attracting both sides to him in a frenzy of effort. While the battle briefly centered on the downed soldier, Renald was able to cat-step behind the headman's lodge and surprise the old man where he stood.

Yet knocking him to the ground and holding him at gunpoint failed to bring about the camp submission Renald sought. For a short while the headman's predicament seemed to go unnoticed, except by the wailing women inside the tepee. But inside they stayed. Perhaps it was acknowledged by the headman's family that they were safer with the paleface among them. Lying parallel on the ground, both the chief and Renald wound up observing the unfolding tragedy as mere spectators.

The mounted soldiers, crisscrossing the encampment in waves, continued scattering the men, shooting horses, collapsing tepees, demolishing wikiups, knocking women and children aside, and shooting at anybody with a weapon; but in doing so more of their mounts went down, and more soldiers with them. Smoke filled the air. The ground was soon littered with wounded men and dead or dying animals.

For his part, Chance, still atop his black charger, was attempting to break through to the Hermann boys. Between him and them was a wall hastily formed by overturned buckboards, barrels, and sledges, and from behind it the enemy fired volley after volley of lead and arrows. More cavalry mounts went down around him.

Meantime, the Indians were suffering from the distraction of Renald holding their elder hostage off to the side. At one point, a warrior managed to work his way around the head tepee, just as Renald had done. Getting behind Renald unnoticed, the Apache was hauling back to impale him with a buffalo pike when a gunshot stopped him. He collapsed onto Renald's shoulders and the spearhead pierced the trembling ground. Twice in just minutes, Renald's life had been saved. This time 10th Troop's Sergeant Neely received his look of gratitude as Renald shrugged off the warrior's limp body.

Then, following distant gunfire, came the rumble of the pony herd let loose on the plains, doubtless a devastating blow to Apache morale.

Before long, a pair of warriors dragged the Hermann boys kicking and scratching out of the fray. Renald saw it happen. Unable to get a clean shot from behind the headman, he watched helplessly as the Apache men pistol-whipped the brothers into unconsciousness and loaded them crosswise onto a couple of ponies. Determination got him back on his feet. Leaving the chief where he lay, he gained purchase of a riderless cavalry mount. As he spurred the animal forward, the tribesmen finished lashing the boys down with sinew strings. They leaped onto their own mounts and lurched toward the sunset with the boys in tow. A second pair of warriors rode close behind as escort.

Sergeant Chance spotted Renald's drive through camp. He whirled his mount and galloped after him. Meantime, the bulk of 10th Troop under Captain Norton's command came plunging through the trees with bugle blaring and guns blazing, scattering what was left of the Apache defense. After that, a vigorously contested raid became the piecemeal slaughter of the Northern People.

* * *

Thanks to a twilight glow, the twisting path was still negotiable at a gallop. When Renald and Chance paused at the rimrock, they spotted the fleeing, shadowy riders and their human chattel as the small party reached a flat stretch of ground below, beyond which lay a pine forest; but before starting down after them, their attention was drawn south by a massive hoof-rumble—the pony herd surging over the rolling prairie. Renald spurred himself again into the lead with Chance following closely. At their unencumbered speed, they would overtake the slower-moving riders before they vanished into the dark timber. The tribesmen concluded the same, and the escorting pair suddenly reversed direction to meet their pursuers head on. For Renald and Chance, there was no time to stake out a position. They simply charged downhill.

War cries arose ahead.

As the advancing riders closed in, Renald observed that one held a rifle. But unlike the Comanche, the Apache were not adept at shooting mounted. If the pair didn't dismount to fire their weapons, they would all collide.

Each side began firing wildly before impact. Renald's mount took a round or two and slammed chest-first to the ground, snapping forelegs and shattering ribs. Able to clear the saddle, Renald landed in a swell of dust. He heard the twang of a bowstring. A feeling of pressure high on his chest followed, and with it the sounds of splitting tissue and cracking bone. The impact drove him back against the shoulder of his thrashing horse.

Meantime, Chance had crashed headlong into the rifle-wielding rider, sending his opponent tumbling backward into the meat grinder of his pony's deadly hooves. Now, reining toward Renald, Chance saw him dispatch his attacker with a single pistol shot to the head. Renald slumped forward. Chance dismounted, grabbed the fallen Apache's long gun, and leapt to Renald's side, where he first put down the man's broken horse with it. Next, he set the weapon aside and gently propped Renald against the saddle flaps.

"You know the routine," said Chance, eliciting a grim nod from his partner. He took hold of the arrow protruding from Renald's back while Renald braced it in a double grip above the entry point. Straining with effort, Chance broke the head off with a crack. Renald pulled out the blood-coated remainder. Each discarded their ends with looks of disgust.

Chance ripped open Renald's bloodied shirt. "You're lucky," he concluded. He untied his yellow scarf, bunched it, and thrust it into the wound.

Renald winced and caught Chance's conflicted stare. "Go get 'em, Tops," he said.

Chance nodded. "Be back shortly."

And he was gone.

* * *

Three years later, Karl Hermann passed by the old family homestead. He was now called "Endah"—or White Boy. It was almost sunup and he and his band of warriors were leading stolen horses back to camp. Cinched to his saddle was a freshly cut scalp.

Between the thickly wooded area from which they had come and these rotting corn fields was the abandoned house. The dark sight unexpectedly moved him. What had become of his parents? His brother?

Endah reined his pony to a halt, surprising his companions. He pointed toward the broken windows. "I lived there," he told them. "I can see my parents as if it were yesterday."

After exchanging glances, one of the group exclaimed, "Go! Go to them."

Another said, "You try hard, but you aren't one of us. Go!"

The third asked, "Didn't you have a brother?"

For an instant Endah considered the prospect of just riding into town, no matter his appearance or the night's raid. It wasn't a thought he seriously entertained, just a what-if scenario, a kind of boyish power fantasy. He could get a whole lot of attention. But his life on the plains was rich and full and exciting. Viewing his former home again, he recalled the endless chores, his parents' ceaseless toils, their strictness, their detachment— and finally he remembered his father's temper. He consumed a breath of air like it was a rare freedom, recognizing that he favored the warmth of his adoptive father and the embrace of the medicine man.

"I had a brother," he answered. "He was unlucky. His bindings broke and they got him back."

He swung his pony around and took the lead as they galloped onto the frontier with their plunder.

Chapter Two

When Tops Chance marched into his commander's sparse office at Fort Richardson, Lieutenant Colonel John Davidson was reading the newspaper, his feet on the desk. Chance stepped forward, waving a telegraph sheet. "Just off the wire, sir. A white warrior was sighted down in Loyal Valley."

Davidson jerked his boots off the desk and rose straight up, his cheeks flushed. "Loyal Valley? In Mason County? That could be Karl Hermann!" He dropped the *Democrat* like it was old news. "Raiding party?"

Chance thrust the message into his hand. "Wife of the deceased said it was Karl done it."

Davidson read the message, blinked, and crumpled it in his fist. "One man's life for a few horses. That boy's thumbing his nose at us."

Chance squared himself, chest out. "Respectfully, sir, I'd like to finish the job."

"You mean go after Karl?" Davidson shook his head. "With peace talks underway at Washington we can't risk another bloody mess."

"Bloody mess, sir?"

"You know what I mean. With C Captain on family leave, I'd have to send you out with Captain Norton and A Company."

"I got no objections reporting to Captain Norton again." Chance raised his chin with pride. "Got me the Medal of Honor, didn't it?"

"And you deserved it for redeeming Karl's brother, but the after-action report made for grim reading." Davidson began to pace. "The Apaches haven't forgotten what Norton did to them—those that live to remember it."

Chance stiffened defensively. "It was kill or be killed, sir."

Smoothing his chin whiskers, Davidson responded, "I know that. But women, children—elders?" The unsaid criticism was of Captain Norton's leadership, not of Chance's. Chance had done what he had to do, Norton endlessly more. "Best to avoid provocation," he concluded with deliberate vagueness.

"How's the *Rangers* gonna react if we sit still, sir?"

"The Rangers will do nothing. If hostilities break out and those talks break down, there'll be hell to pay with the governor." Davidson clapped Chance's stripes. "Good morning, by the way! Coffee?"

His orderly absent, Davidson himself did the pouring from the battered kettle he brought to every posting. He led Chance out onto the porch. They took their seats in a couple of chairs overlooking the windswept parade grounds, as was their routine. A year prior, the 10th Cavalry had been transferred to this post from Fort Sill in Indian Territory. Except for the commissioned officers—and Sergeant Tyler—this was a buffalo soldier troop. Hence, other post commanders called Colonel Davidson "Black Jack." At first it was simply a ribbing, but his own men soon adopted the practice, and coming from them the moniker was endearing.

Because the Red River campaign of '74 had netted most of the holdout Comanche and Kiowa, and this post was far from Apache country, Black Jack now found himself with a lot of time on his hands, his men grown weary of the endless drilling and uneventful patrols. The fort was soon to be decommissioned, and in fact C Troop's captain would not be coming back from family leave—only Davidson knew this for the moment. It was a time of change, of repositioning the army's resources to meet current demands, south and further west. Soon Davidson would be taking charge of Fort Custer in Montana, and Chance would be following Captain Norton to Fort Concho with a slew of recruits. Other members of the 10th had been assigned to forts along the Rio Grande to help quell Indian raiding from Mexico.

Chance, a Baltimore tobacconist's assistant before the War Between the States, pulled a pair of cigars from inside his topcoat. "If you please, sir …"

Davidson happily reached across the small table separating them. "Enough with the *sirs*," he chided. "It's just the two of us here, Tops."

Commander and sergeant lit up and exhaled luxuriously.

"You know I don't blame you for that raid on the Northern People," Davidson offered. "If I did, I wouldn't have approved the commendation. But what started out as a rescue operation ended in a massacre. Norton commanded like General Custer at the Washita that day, and he should remember what happened to Custer the next time he used those tactics." But Davidson avoided speaking worse of his remaining captain, or of the slain general whose honorary post he was to command. He blew a long plume of smoke. "We've been through a lot together, Tops—accomplished a lot. In a profession where men often advance from displays of bravery, I've always relied on—and admired—your circumspection."

"Thank you, sir."

"But then you go storming in here about Karl Hermann as if it's war! Why?"

Chance smoothed his mustache—a confirmation to his longtime commander that he was holding something back.

"Well?"

Chance's chest rose and fell. "There's a girl gone missing too …"

Davidson turned up his lips, reading his subordinate. "You mean the Negro girl down at Fort Chadbourne?"

"Yessir, last month. Sergeant Neely's girl."

"*Ex*-sergeant Neely," Davidson emphasized. He frowned. "As I recall, he left the troop to become Tom Odom's ramrod." Asquint through the smoke, he added, "Damn shame, his losing a child because of it."

"Their only child," replied Chance. "Her name is Emma."

"Emma *was* her name," Davidson replied. Then, "*Neely* … Didn't he fight in the Northern People raid?"

Chance raised himself up in his chair. "A slug from his revolver stopped a brave fixing to spear Mr. Renald."

Davidson nodded. "I recall it from Norton's report. Well, what attempts has Neely made to get her back?" Davidson knew better than to inquire if the army had attempted to find her. The U.S. Cavalry didn't deploy for lost Negroes, hence the Indians seldom attempted to ransom them back.

"Mr. Odom allowed him a two-week search, was all," Chance answered. "Nobody knew if it was Apache, Comanche, or

Kiowa done it—so they rode south, west, finally north." When Davidson offered nothing in reply, he continued. "Them hostiles make slaves of black girls."

Black Jack leaned forward with irritation. "It ain't a fair world, Tops. It just ain't. Stop thinking like a concerned Negro and remember you're a soldier." He rolled the cigar between his fingers, studying it. "Indians never used to make property of people. They learned it from us."

"*Us?*" Chance's reply was uncharacteristically short—in both senses of the word.

Davidson reacted with a look of surprise at the utterance. Switching his view to the empty marching grounds, he avoided his sergeant's hurt. "So you're hoping a pursuit of Karl Hermann might lead us to her, this Emma."

"I'm not the only one who didn't finish the Hermann job."

"Don't push it, Sergeant." Davidson tapped his cigar on a clay ashtray between them. "We all invested in finding Karl Hermann. Do you think I'm content with the outcome?"

"I didn't mean you, sir. I meant Scott Renald."

"Renald!" Davidson groaned at the thought of the retired civilian scout, a Comanche speaker—not one with Apache expertise. "I don't like where this is leading, Tops."

"He's just outside of Fort Worth, sir."

"Are you suggesting he volunteer? Renald's breeding Morgans for God's sake!"

"Ain't it worth inquiring at least?"

Davidson sat up. "You've got *some pluck* supposing Renald would risk his life for a … for a …" He stopped himself.

For a Negro girl?

If Chance was troubled by the implication, he didn't show it. Perhaps Davidson meant that Renald wouldn't put his life at risk for a full-blown white Apache. He took a long, easy drag while Davidson tapped his armrest in consternation. Somewhere, a horse neighed.

Finally, Black Jack rose with a huff. His back turned, he confessed, "Many a night I've prayed for Karl Hermann."

Chance followed him to his feet, leaving his cigar in the ashtray. "Me too. Lately, though, I been praying for *her*. Emma Neely."

This brought Davidson to pivot and face him—but Black Jack's expression was tender, anguished. After a moment, he said, "I'll need to inform Karl's widowed mother in Fort Worth right away—don't want her learning about it from tomorrow's papers. Given the details of the raid, it'll be worse than reporting his death."

"Won't you feel better about it if you check with Mr. Renald first? About Karl Hermann, I mean, sir."

"I notice those *sirs* are back!" replied Davidson, brandishing his cigar.

Chance leaned forward. "They helping some?"

"The *sirs* or the cigars? This is about that boy and his mother. But I'm not saying I won't pay Renald a visit."

Chance cracked a smile. "How about some company on the road, sir? Long ride there and back."

Davidson eyed him aslant. "I'll bring a book," he said.

"Me too," Chance responded with a satisfied smile.

* * *

"A case like Karl Hermann's is rare indeed," Davidson observed on their bumpy coach ride to Fort Worth. "No marshals heading into Apache lands for him, and no bounty's being offered. What are the courts to do with such a case?" He shook his head at the complexities.

Both he and Chance, sitting opposite each other in the drafty interior, had brought along reading material for the journey. Occasionally they heard whip cracks and exhortations from the driver's seat. Lying unopened in Davidson's lap was a copy of De B. Randolph Keim's *Sheridan's Views on the Indian Question*, while on the seat next to Chance lay a copy of Ophelia Wheatman's *My Life Among the Apache and the Mohave*.

"Poor kid," Chance responded. "Maybe that's why nobody's still looking. Karl ain't no captive no more. But he *is* a victim."

"Is he?" With the morning chill lifting, Davidson tugged his gloves off by the gauntlets. "After this event, there isn't a man in Texas who'd consider him anything but a hostile," he said. "The time is coming for all the holdout Apache, and when it does, Karl would be safer on a reservation."

"And if we do manage to bring him in?"

"I suppose he'd be sent to the Kirkby to get the wild out. Same as Laura Little was."

Recalling the unusual case of Laura Little, Chance responded, "That Dr. Kirkby sure didn't get the wild outta her! She went over him like a—well, like an Indian!" A former Comanche captive, Laura Little once broke out of the Kirkby Sanitarium to search for the Indian son she was forced to leave behind. Scott Renald, finding her again a hostage—but this time of the allied Tonkawa tribe—liberated her and then led her search. During their escape, he killed the headman and later she killed a Tonk army scout, triggering an army board of inquiry.

The mention of Laura Little made Davidson squirm in his seat. He stretched his legs crossways in the space between them, saying nothing.

"You said them cases don't go to trial," Chance continued, "but we put Miss Little on the stand."

"*I* put her on the stand," Davidson answered. "A way of clearing her, not convicting her. The judge's ruling came straight from Dr. Kirkby's professional opinion. *Acculturation,* he called it."

"Downright kind of the doc!—after she hogtied and robbed him."

Davidson shifted his weight on the thin cushion. "Those were the actions of a Comanche squaw, at least that's how the judge ruled, conveniently." He sighed. "However one judges Laura Little, she's no charlatan like that Ophelia Wheatman you're reading about." Frowning, he indicated Chance's book. "Miss Wheatman lectures all over the country about her experience with the Indians like it was downright hell—while at the same time insisting she was never raped. Never raped and never married! We're supposed to believe that. Just look at that cover illustration, all prim and proper—except for those tattoos on her chin and cheeks. Which edition is that? *My Life Among the Apache and the Mohave?* Well, when it first came out it was just *My Life Among the Apache.* No mention of the Mohave anyplace. Know why? Because those facial marks are the brand of a Mohave *wife.*"

Holding the book now, Chance confessed, "Wife? I don't follow, sir."

His commander explained. "The Apache sold her to the Mohave, but to this day she denies being married to their chief, Espanesay—denies bearing him a daughter. It is said that the girl is living on the reservation right now, a motherless child." Davidson scoffed. "Far from being a Mohave slave, Miss Wheatman was their queen."

With real wonder in his voice, and with only a hint of bitterness, Chance replied, "Damned if I ever knew somebody who lied about being a slave in the reverse."

Davidson nodded. "She's ashamed to admit she never claimed her daughter like Laura Little claimed her son."

Chance tapped the book. "Says here on the cover it's sold thirty thousand copies—thirty thousand and one." With a grimace, he tossed it back onto the seat. "If only I hadn't left Karl behind," he added, somberly, focused on the prairie beyond the jittering window.

"Don't think that way, Tops. You knew when to stop. What if you'd taken an arrow pursuing Karl into that forest? Renald might be dead and *both* children would be lost. Hell, you'd be dead too!"

Chance turned back with a grave expression. "How've others like Karl done?"

"After being restored to society?" Davidson huffed. "It's never a happy story. We saw it with Adolph Korn. We saw it with Rudolph Fischer. Easier for people to accept a damaged woman than some murderous man. One youth who came back a Cheyenne warrior was lynched for it—the mob did what the law won't. No, Karl Hermann is better off where he is! I expect Renald will say the same."

"At least we're giving him a try," said Chance wistfully, thinking of lost Emma Neely.

Davidson leaned forward and slapped his trooper's knee with his glove. "You're welcome, Sergeant! Now read that there story book …"

Chapter Three

Arcing southeast, after several hours the coach crossed a broad cattle trail stretching westward from Fort Worth. Here, a merchant heading out in a Conestoga wagon confirmed the location of Scott Renald's spread, and within an hour his A-frame roof came into view, poking out from a copse of ash and old-growth pines. A bearded Mexican man in an airy white blouse met them where the driveway circled in front of the house.

Davidson's top-coated whip assisted him out of the carriage, followed by Chance.

"Good afternoon, *señores,*" said the ranch hand, looking surprised. "We were expecting a coach, but not an army one." He appraised the frills of Davidson's uniform. "A lieutenant colonel, I see."

This elicited a look of curiosity from the chin-whiskered commander. Was the Mexican a former soldier?

Chance sucked air, then announced, "Lieutenant Colonel John Davidson, 10th Cavalry, Fort Richardson. Calling on Mr. Renald …"

"*Señor* Renald is happy to receive you. *Por favor,* follow me."

"At ease, Private," Chance told their driver.

To the loudening hacks of wood-cutting, Renald's ranch hand led them along a flat stone path outlining the single-story house. Rounding a corner, they were faced with the V-tapered back of a browned, shirtless man, the light playing off his working muscles as he brought down the axe with yet another crack. Beyond him lay the corral and stables.

"*Señor* Renald!" called the worker. "Some men visit you."

Gripping the axe in one hand and wiping his brow with the back of the other, Scott Renald turned their way, blue eyes glinting, silver hair shining, and the cratered scar below his left shoulder shadowy in the noonday light.

"What a surprise! Black Jack Davidson … Sergeant Chance …" He strode forward, perfectly balanced despite the heavy tool in his grasp. He pumped both men's hands as they exchanged greetings.

"Looking fit, Scott," Davidson offered. "You put me to shame."

"Try chopping your own wood," Renald responded. He handily passed the axe to his helper, who accepted it in a double grip. "This here's Luís, my foreman."

Struggling with the weight of the axe, Luís said, "*Mucho gusto conocerles, señores.*"

To Davidson, Renald remarked, "You once chased his army into Mexico. Happily, Luís found his way back."

They all chuckled, including Luís. "I like it better here!" he responded. "Please excuse me—I have much to do." He lumbered off in the direction of the tool shed.

Renald's grin faded and he crossed his thick forearms as if bracing for a problem. "And the purpose of your visit is? …"

Davidson met his gaze. "Scott, the elder Hermann boy's been sighted with a band of Apache. Seems he took a scalp back home in Mason. Some horses too."

"Do or die," Renald replied. "Taken boys who don't adapt to Indian ways don't live long."

"We're about to break the news to Mrs. Hermann," said Chance.

"I thought house calls are made only to report a death."

"Same difference," Davidson grunted.

Renald sighed. "She'll feel worse about his not coming home than about his carving out that scalp." He held Davidson's gaze before his countenance lightened. "Let's step out of the sun and get you men some refreshment."

Heading into his covered patio, he swiped a red flannel shirt from the back of a chair at the head of a mahogany table set for four. He led them into a window-lit parlor around which three rooms and a kitchen were situated. Buttoning up, he invited the men to sit down. They took their seats in a pair of upholstered armchairs facing a free-standing iron fireplace whose pipe ran through the ceiling. Adorning the walls were framed pictures of horses, not people—with one exception, Chance noted. After Renald disappeared into the adjoining kitchen, Tops got to his feet and approached the grainy tintype of a well-dressed adolescent boy embracing Renald around the waist and projecting a proud smile at the camera.

Clasping his sergeant's cap against his chest, he whispered, "Is that Talks White? …"

"He's called Jimmy now," Davidson answered. Born to Laura Little and the half-blood Comanche headman Talking Moon, Jimmy had adapted to living white in place of the defining first hunt that would have made him a Comanche man. His paternal grandmother, a captive herself, was Scott Renald's late sister.

With Davidson nodding knowingly, the sergeant rejoined his commander. In the background were the sounds of Renald's hasty rumblings in the kitchen. He soon returned with a tin tray, on it two glasses of water and ceramic appetizer bowls filled with nuts.

"Thanking you kindly, Scott," Chance exclaimed as he transferred the stuff to the coffee table between Davidson and himself. "Almonds besides!"

"Luís orders 'em from south of the border." Renald popped one in his mouth. "We do the roasting here."

Without further pause the two hungry officers reached for the snacks.

"There's lunch Mexican style if you can wait. Jimmy and his folks are expected any time now. He's staying with me through the weekend."

The men exchanged looks. The prospect of a reunion was enticing, but they would find lunch in town. "Our man outside is as eager as we are to reach Fort Worth," Davidson replied.

"Suit yourselves," replied Renald. "Just give me a minute …"

While Renald returned the tray to the kitchen he called back to them the story of how, after his recuperation, he built the house and stables with the help of Luís and his sons. "Still much to do," he conceded, re-entering the room with a glass of water for himself. He propped a boot on the side of the stove and gulped some water down. "How about your wives, your kids? Adjusting to Fort Richardson?"

Davidson responded for both of them. "Everybody's just fine, Scott. Quiet out there since you brought the Comanche in. Wouldn't you say, Tops?"

Chance nodded. "The troop's getting downright antsy."

"Good to hear," Renald responded. "Patrols will be a thing of the past."

"I'll be assuming command of Fort Custer next month," Davidson added. "Tops here is joining Captain Norton at Fort Concho. Our troop numbers are down."

"Going where the action is, the both of you—north, and further west." With his boot still planted on the side of the stove, Renald straightened himself to address their hitherto unspoken request. "I'm not interested, John," he said with a sigh.

"Scott, you haven't even heard us out."

Shaking his head, Renald replied, "You'll have to find somebody else. Somebody who knows the Apache, who talks Spanish at least."

"We did. Two years ago. After your injury, we sent an agent out with two White Mountain scouts."

"And?"

Davidson shrugged. "I presume they all met the Great Spirit."

"What salesmanship! And now you want me to go? I prefer to spend my retirement alive."

"Think of his mother, Scott. Raising Freddie alone in a one-roomer above the post office."

"Is that where she is ..." Renald lowered his voice. "I do think of her, and of what our failure cost her. But I got a little business here breeding horses. And ..." He gestured toward a door on the far side of the fireplace. "I got a room there just for Jimmy, like I would for my own grandchild. No, sir. I'm not going. Best let Karl Hermann scamper back into the thicket." He drained his glass and set it down between the two men. "I went out for white people, not Indians. By now Karl Hermann is a full-fledged Apache. You know it as well as I do."

Davidson got to his feet, with Chance closely following his lead. "I don't blame you, Scott. Tops here wanted to ride out after him, but I can't—"

"No need to explain. I understand. And I know about the peace talks."

They chatted awhile before Renald led them out on the front porch, which opened onto a lawn partially shaded by Texas ash, a silent scene but for the odd avian chirp or song. In some shade to their left, the army private was dozing, his head supported by his clasped hands, his features hidden beneath his visor. Under another tree to their right, the pair of lead horses, still tethered to the coach, were stamping their hooves and swatting flies. A water bucket had been placed before them, doubtless Luís' doing. Chance descended the steps and prodded the driver with the side of his boot.

The sounds of wheels and hooves grinding up the dirt drive reached them, and soon a second carriage behind a team of horses broke into view. On its driver's box sat two silhouettes, one of them riding shotgun. Today in the area of Fort Worth there was no risk of falling victim to banditry or Indians, so the presence of a shotgun beside the whip was purely for show, like wearing a sidearm in town. A curious sight to Colonel Davidson. He moved toward the approaching vehicle with Renald and Chance following. The carriage halted where the army men and their host stood.

"Damned if it ain't the whole gang!" droned a voice from within.

The buggy door burst open, and filling the frame was none other than the burly Cole Hawker, owner-operator of the Big C-H. Squeezed into a jacket, vest, and shiny shoes—no hat on him—the polish of his person came as nothing less than a shock to Chance, who remembered him as a down-on-his-luck, mangy skinner. Even his beard seemed combed. Colonel Davidson was, in fact, responsible for Hawk's newfound prosperity, having awarded him the army beef contract for his part in finding and returning Laura Little.

"Black Jack Davidson, no less!" Hawk exclaimed.

As he lowered himself to the ground, young Jimmy replaced him in the doorframe.

In the three short years since Renald first laid eyes on the fair-haired, rosy-cheeked "Talks White," his great-nephew had transformed from a so-called white Indian, who slept on the ground, into a child of this culture, who slept in a four-poster bed. "Uncle Scott!" the nine-year-old cried, leaping out. He crashed into Renald's adoring embrace, almost toppling him.

While Renald and Jimmy were thus entangled, Hawk threw his arm around a rather stiff Colonel Davidson. Only Hawk's appearance was refined; otherwise, he was as uncouth and provocative as ever. Next, he crushed Chance's hand in his, observing, "And here we got the *black* in Jack!"

From Chance, this factual observation caused no more than an amused grin. Hawk, now holding each trooper by the shoulder, told the commander, "In this fella you done brung your better half!"

Renald saved Davidson from responding to Hawk. With a nod toward the carriage, he said, "So did *you,* I see …"

It was a reference to Laura Little Hawker, the ex-governor's niece, who was presently stepping down—unassisted—from the vehicle. Chance hastened to her, and though she accepted his helping hand with a quick smile, a look of annoyance swiftly replaced it. After all, the last time she'd seen these men assembled was at her inquest for murder.

Still favoring pants over skirts, today she wore trousers and boots under a knee-length grey top dress. A touch of rouge brought out her cheekbones, and her long blond hair was worn braided down her back. Groomed and clothed thus, she could have sat for tea quite as naturally as vaulting herself onto the back of somebody's horse and thieving it.

Davidson came forward, content to shake off her husband's bear paw. "A distinct pleasure, Mrs. Hawker …" He saluted with flourish before removing his hat, then bowed deep enough to expose his salt and pepper-fringed bald spot.

Without a return curtsy, she simply replied, "Colonel …"

"John to you, ma'am."

"*Colonel* to me, thank you."

Her coolness toward him did not surprise. Besides having put her on the stand, it was also Davidson's doing that Talking Moon—her former husband—was a perpetual visitor to their ranch outside Fort Worth, as often to see Jimmy as to sell Hawk cheap reservation cattle. This arrangement reflected a rapidly changing world full of bitter sacrifices, awkward accommodations, perpetual coping, and—yes— new opportunities.

Collecting herself, she glanced pointedly from man to man with her piercing green eyes. "You'll forgive me if I seem startled. To what do we owe your presence, Colonel?" Guardedly, she added, "Something about? …" She raised her chin toward Jimmy, wrapped in Renald's bent arm.

"No, ma'am," came the reply.

Nevertheless, Laura seemed to stiffen. "Are we all dining together, then?"

Davidson replied, "The table's set for four. Duty calls in town, ma'am."

"A pity," she said with mock sincerity.

Renald jumped in for Jimmy's sake, gesturing first toward Davidson, then Tops. "Do you remember these men from the day your new life started?"

The boy blinked his brown eyes under a thready nest of brown hair that shone bronze as he tilted his head in the direct sunlight. Like his half-blood father, Talking Moon, he was big-boned and tall, standing nearly chest-height beside the tall Renald. "I think I remember one of them, Uncle," he said. "The man who separated me from my father."

To this Davidson cleared his throat, then responded, "Well, I couldn't divide you in two, now could I? But our peace terms included that pass your father travels on to see you."

"Done set him up in business too," Hawk added.

Davidson remained fixed on Jimmy, no doubt struck by how adapted he appeared. A true wonder. But the boy's education had begun in the Indian camp with his mother and grandmother, once a schoolteacher. "I bet you're good in school, young man," said the commander.

"Top of his class last year!" This from his proud mother.

"Well, what do you say?" he exclaimed to the boy.

Rather than blushing, Jimmy replied, "Why do you act surprised, sir? *I'm smart.*"

Davidson took this in stride. "Not surprising at all, knowing your folks."

"The three of us," Hawk clarified.

As the interaction continued, Sergeant Chance edged himself backward unnoticed, one careful step at a time. When, finally, he had withdrawn to their waiting coach, he climbed into the cabin to retrieve the Ophelia Wheatman book. Inserted in its pages was a secret a message for Scott Renald—but any chance of slipping it to him was dashed when his commander started for the vehicle with Renald at his side. Behind them, the Hawkers were retiring into the house, Cole chortling at something.

"Take care up there in Sioux country, you hear?" Renald was saying.

Davidson paused beside the vehicle and locked eyes with his old friend. "Just give it some thought, Scott. I mean about Karl." The commander then turned on his heel toward the open carriage door and—as luck would have it—caught sight of the volume his top sergeant was holding at his side. Davidson smoothed his whiskers thoughtfully. Nothing more.

Offering the book to Renald, Chance met his gaze. "The colonel ain't kind to it," he said, striking a cryptic tone, "but have yourself a look inside, Scott …"

Pokerfaced, Renald wished them luck in Fort Worth.

* * *

The coach plunged down the drive with a drum of hooves, and now stepping toward his front door, Renald paged through the curious gift. Stories of captivity were always entrancing to him—whether on the whole honest or not—but just what had made Chance push this one on him? The answer came as a card-sized item slipped from between its pages and fluttered down to the welcome mat. Retrieving it with a bend of stiff knees, Renald recognized it as a tintype akin to those he'd carried on his searches. Only this one was of a Negro child, a girl perhaps four years in age.

He flipped it over and read, *Emma Neely needs you too.*

Chapter Four

The spot was moving rapidly toward him over the brightening prairie. A bold, arrogant advance—one initiated either by a keen eye or by an undetected system of alerts.

"So that's how it is," Renald muttered to himself.

A plainsman without Renald's way with a Winchester would've been saying his prayers just about now. The enemy was relying on the traditional scare-and-chase tactic that normally sent white men scattering. It was Renald's first test of strength this time out. Without taking his eyes off the incoming object, he reached forward to draw his rifle and alighted from his saddle. He pushed a knee into the ground and raised the gunsight to his cheek. His army-issue mount instinctively stepped back.

The spot grew and grew against the amber backdrop of open country at dawn. No yelps, no whoops, just bird flutter amid the hoof-pounding. Brash and plumb stupid, his opponent was riding right into a torrent of lead. Too easy. Renald scanned his desolate surroundings, but detected nothing else. Returning to his focus, he watched as the blotch sharpened, expanded, and rose in his view until he was seeing in it *two* targets. Now in range, they divided, breaking to each side. The Apache were shrewd, and this close-in they were probably Lipan.

Such tactics worked against most men, but Renald wasn't fazed. It all depended on his engaging one attacker at a time with lightning efficiency. Swinging his rifle to the left, he squinted down the sight to prevent blinking. *Saddle*, he observed—*this one's mounted on a saddle. Curious.* He sucked air and squeezed off a single round. The rider slumped and dropped. But Renald was no longer watching. Such was his confidence with a long gun that he was already pivoting toward the remaining opponent, who—warned by the gunshot—was now galloping in for a direct attack.

Another saddle mount, he noticed.

This warrior, concealed behind a shield, made for a difficult shot. Renald could surely hit the target, but taut buffalo hide was a mighty defense. If he wasted rounds trying to penetrate it, his opponent would trample him.

As the rumble of hoofbeats increased to a roar, he was forced to shoot the pony.

A cloud of dust went up as she came crashing down. The warrior raced forward through the billow on foot, a relentless desert predator. Renald fired one useless shot after another against the angled hide shield. Now shrilly war whooping, the attacker cleared the hundred feet between them in seconds. The bold charge was meant to reduce Renald's superiority with the rifle. Rising to a crouch, he braced himself for impact. At close quarters a dagger was an Indian's deadliest weapon, and Renald had to prepare for one. In the space of a breath or two he must choose a defensive measure. He could meet the onslaught with his Winchester clutched horizontally between two hands—a buffer—but that wouldn't leave a hand free to deal with a knife or a blow. Or he could discard his rifle to free his left hand while he drew his sidearm with his right. But that would leave his long gun within reach of his attacker.

Or, at close range, he could try once more with the saddle gun—this time, with a height advantage, adjusting for the angle of the shield.

He hauled up the rifle and blasted the animal hide straight on. With physics now in his favor, a hole appeared in the hide and the figure behind it was thrown onto his back, the smoking shield falling over his chest and face. A bend of the knees in baggy pants signaled the fallen warrior's only attempt to rise, and he collapsed with a single groan. Renald lowered the gun. The Apache's raven hair was fanned on the ground beyond the shield's rim, and in his inert right hand he held the anticipated blade. Renald sensed that he was merely unconscious. Working fast, he took no chances. He set a boot on the warrior's wrist and pried the blade away.

What slender fingers, he thought. Garbed in chinaman's trousers and a billowy white shirt fit for a Mexican, even for an Apache this brave was slight of build. A mere youth? Renald tossed the knife halfway to his own horse, then pulled the warrior's short gun and, rising, slipped it under his belt. With his attacker unconscious and disarmed, Renald allowed his eyes to search the surroundings for further signs of danger. Beyond the dead heap of the horse he detected nothing.

Now, Winchester at the ready, he approached the first attacker to fall, who lay face down on the turf. At his approach, the pony shied away, leaving him a clean shot should the warrior have a surprise left in him. Grasping him by the shoulder, Renald rolled the man over—then stepped back in astonishment. A woman's unblinking eyes stared up at him as her graceful body settled onto its back, a trickle of blood running from lips to ear.

"That's a first," he remarked aloud, "a squaw equipped like a brave." Glancing back with suspicion at the other body, he added, "And I have a fair idea who you two are …" He bent down and unbuckled the woman warrior's gunbelt, then pulled it toward him as he rose and slapped it across his shoulder. Next, he reached for the pony's bridle. With the animal in tow, he returned to the wounded other. This time he wasn't surprised when a flip of the shield revealed yet another woman.

Above her right eye was a gash she would be proud of.

* * *

Renald's deadly encounter with the two fighting women wasn't a mere coincidence. Before he set out, Davidson's office had received intelligence of a major Lipan Apache encampment southeast of Fort Concho at the Kickapoo Springs. For now, the army was leaving it alone in the hope that a treaty would result from the negotiations at Washington. To Renald, the moment had seemed right to make contact. But what did he know? He was a *Comanche* expert.

Strapped belly-down on the surviving Indian pony, the handcuffed and unconscious woman remained still throughout the morning, and only began groaning and shifting in the late afternoon. They'd come a long way since Renald left her partner's body in a shallow grave in the open country behind them. When it seemed his prisoner was on the verge of reviving, he stopped to make camp. The sun was burning gold in the sky ahead, silhouetting the mesquite bushes before them.

Both she and her friend had been packing army bedrolls strapped behind their saddles, the spoils of some deadly raid, perhaps. He made her bed. A yard away, he unrolled his own army-issue rubber mat. Next, he approached the nervous dapple grey on which she was slung. Though the grey first sidestepped, when the animal sensed that Renald was attempting to unburden her, she let him do it. Unstrapped, the woman slipped off the mount like a burlap sack into Renald's arms. He bent his knees to absorb the weight. With effort, he lay her lithe form sideways on the blanket, then eased her onto her back. As her body settled, he stepped away to have a look. Her shoulder-length hair was divided in the Apache fashion and flattened at the roots by a band of embroidered cloth. Her eyebrows were as trim as a lady's, eyelashes as fine and long as golden barrel cactus petals. Between her high cheekbones, her broad nose lacked elegance—but a man looked past noses—and beneath her rather full lips, a boyishly cleft chin added to her allure.

He returned to his chores, a hand on the small of his back.

By dusk she began regaining consciousness, and Renald trickled some whiskey from his bottle through her lips. Gagging, she raised her shackled hands. He sat back down, his right side warmed by the campfire in the rising desert chill.

Her curved lashes fluttered. Opening her eyes, she at once gleaned her situation. She leapt to her feet and tried to bolt, only to fall hard on her face. He'd bound her ankles too.

Cross-legged opposite her, Renald remarked, "You're either the fabled Lipan called Chivatá or the fabled Mescalero, Nalen. If you're Chivatá, they say you speak English."

Cheek to the ground, she hesitated, as if thinking. Then she began writhing in the dirt in an attempt to right herself. He rose and grabbed her under the arms, trying to help. When she attempted to bite his hand, he released her in a swell of dust. Her eyes flared as she wriggled into a sitting position.

"Have it your way," he said, sighing. He stepped around the glowing embers to his black charger and detached one of his canteens. He dropped it at her bent knees, then helped himself to a cup of coffee from the kettle, fireside.

"I'd offer you some coffee," he said, "but I'm afraid I'd get it back in my face."

She glowered at him, left cheek smudged with dirt.

"I'll take that as confirmation you're Chivatá." He pointed to the canteen. "You should drink." Then he said, "Since I speak hardly a word of Apache—and as much Spanish—I'm gonna assume you understand me." He folded his legs. "You *are* Chivatá, aren't you?"

Nothing.

"It's said that Nalen and Chivatá ride together. Chivatá is supposed to be a real beauty."

She dipped her chin and stared at the ground. Her chest rose and fell.

"You should eat too," he said. "I've got some dried beef and some tins." He sipped his coffee and tried to catch her gaze. "You're not going to talk to me? That's fine, but listen up. When dawn breaks, we're heading straight for the Lipan encampment at the Kickapoo Springs—and then you'll be free. Nobody wants trouble while your chiefs are talking peace with ours. You might've considered that before you rushed me."

In reply, she just glared.

"Drink your water," he said, and got to his feet. "I'll find you that salt beef."

He went to his horse, pulled an oil-stained paper sack from his saddle bag, and glanced across the campfire. She was drinking mightily from the upturned vessel. "Good," he said, returning to her. "Drink as much as you like." He tossed her the sack. "Those strips are pretty tasty. Better eat up, 'cuz you'll sleep with your hands tied behind your back."

She might have understood him, because when he began unbuckling his gun, she partook of the food.

"You'll be needing to do your business," he said, "… take a little tinkle or something." He tossed his gunsling a safe distance away. "So you'll be needing your hands." He came around behind her and told her to get up. When she didn't respond, he grabbed her under the arms. "Be nice," he said in her ear, "… be smart."

She complied, rising to her feet. With his chest pressing against her back, he reached around her slender form, in effect embracing her from behind. A ribbon of hair brushed his cheek.

He unlocked one cuff and quickly stepped back, aware she could swing it wildly. But she was smart, and didn't. He moved away and averted his gaze, and when she was finished, he stepped forward to shackle her again. Without protest, she allowed him to.

"You need anything during the night," he said, "you break your silence—you hear? My name's Renald—or Scott, if that's easier. Goodnight, Chivatá."

Chapter Five

Several weeks before Renald set out on his mission, none other than Ophelia Wheatman had come to Fort Worth on a book tour. Scott was among the first of her readers to arrive at Leary's Booksellers. It was the first in a series of events that would change his mind about pursuing the white warrior. Propped behind the stacks of her memoir in the window was a large, wet plate print of her tattooed visage beneath the eye-catching label "CAPTIVE."

Inside, a bell over the door chiming upon entry, Renald was confronted by a table display not only of Wheatman's book, but of a number of captivity stories that fed the public's enduring hunger for the topic. Some book covers depicted solemn subjects, like Ophelia Wheatman herself, while others were dressed up fancifully like dime store novels, which is how quite a few of them read. Renald first noticed *Three Years among the Comanches*, written by a Texas Ranger once held by the tribe. Other titles included: *An Affecting Narrative of the Captivity and Suffering of Mrs. Mary Smith* and *A Narrative of the Life of Mrs. Mary Jemison*. He found himself picking up a copy of *Narrative of My Captivity among the Sioux Indians* before replacing it with slit eyes for the impossibly long-titled *Narrative of the Perilous Adventures, Miraculous Escapes and Sufferings of Rev. James W. Parker during a Frontier Residence in Texas, of Fifteen Years; with an Impartial Geographical Description of the Climate, Soil, Timber, Water, &c., &c., &c. of Texas; Written by Himself. To Which is Appended a Narrative of the Capture and Subsequent Sufferings of Mrs. Rachel Plummer (His Daughter).*

Renald breathed out as he set the volume down. The Parker-Plummer story was known to just about everybody.

Although most folks on the frontier had lost somebody or knew someone who'd lost somebody to the Indians, the general public still harbored a fascination with the captive's story as if it were some sort of fantastical experience that affected only other people. Renald, having lost family to the Comanche himself—both murdered and abducted—considered any such book questionable entertainment. For him, there was something untoward about selling the story of oneself, particularly if it was spiced with sensational elements, such as Wheatman's cringe-inducing "… and then the savages, reverting from the mangled corpses of my dear parents, cast their vengeful eyes upon my innocent person …" A more truthful text might have called their eyes "lustful," and her person "chaste." While most books of this sort were embellished by their publishers, they tended to spare the former hostage embarrassment or scandal. Ophelia Wheatman's seemed no exception. The bottom line was, you couldn't trust these books.

Beyond the display table was a seating area arranged like a church interior with an aisle down the middle, a dais at the end, and bracketed by walls of books rather than side altars. Renald, who chose to linger behind the last row of seats, was one of the few men in an audience buzzing with restless anticipation. In fact, well before the seven p.m. start time, only standing room remained. With the confines growing increasingly stuffy, the staff propped open the street door and distributed hand fans to those ladies who'd neglected to bring their own. A few extra chairs were produced. Content to remain where he was, Renald resisted the urge to lean on the rolling foot ladder to his right. Frankly, he didn't know what to do with himself in such company, in such a place. Throughout his career, which included service in three wars, he had been too occupied or restless to read much, but intrigued by the seductive, haunting image of its tattooed author on the cover, he'd devoured this book overnight, nodding as much as shaking his head.

Now, scratching the sun-beaten back of his neck, he let his eyes wander from hat to hat, shelf to shelf, gaslight to gaslight. Still no sign of the author. Midway down the row of seats, a man taller even than himself vacated his chair for an elderly woman seeking one. Whiskered and suit-dressed—his watch chain dangling over a practitioner's gut—this not unfamiliar man made his way to the rear.

"Doctor Kirkby ..." said Renald, extending his hand.

The doc's mouth opened dumbly. Then, "Oh, yes, Randolph, isn't it? Reeves, perhaps?"

Renald enjoyed the moment. "Not Randolph, not Reeves—Renald."

"Right! The Indian agent ..."

"Officially a recovery agent—or a 'redeemer,' as we're commonly called. Retired now ..."

"Well, that's disappointing!" Dr. Kirkby replied, pumping Renald's hand. "We have plenty of rooms waiting for those in need."

"Those that can afford them."

"We do have our costs, sir. Collections are taken for those who cannot meet them. Not all our patients are from families as privileged as Laura Little's. I believe we last met at her inquest …"

Renald remembered. "Where you recounted how she helped herself to a partial refund from your billfold, financing her escape. I see you got your ring back."

At this, Dr. Kirkby regarded his wedding band with a sigh, and Renald noted his boulder-sized fist—and yet the big man had been no match for Laura Little. The doctor took the tease in stride. "Mr. Renald, in our institution we have both a curable and an incurable ward. Alas, Miss Little was admitted to the curable ward."

"Everybody makes mistakes," Renald responded.

Ophelia Wheatman had appeared as they spoke. Lithe in a black lace dress, raven-haired and ivory-skinned behind the facial tattoos, she stepped up to the podium. At her side was the proprietor, Mr. Leary—hunched, bespectacled, and yellow-skinned.

Chin raised, Dr. Kirkby remarked, "That little lady has also found her way into our wallets. Quite a success story, beginning with her stay at my sanitarium."

"You got the wild out of her, did you?"

"Hers was a lighter case. She was away only three years."

"Only three years, you say!" Renald lowered his voice. "I read the book. But nobody comes back unscathed." Tapping his temple, he repeated, "Nobody."

Dr. Kirkby opened his mouth to respond but the sound that reached Renald's ears was an "Ah-hem" broadcast by Mr. Leary. The disappointed head doc swallowed his reply with a look of loss. As the host began introducing the speaker, Renald was struck by the famous marks she bore. To his surprise, the spidery pattern that branched over her chin and lower cheeks was turquoise in color, not the charcoal scratchings captured by photography.

Her measured gaze appraising the room, Ophelia Wheatman greeted her audience in a throaty voice, and then commenced professionally with her lecture.

As it happened, Renald, who'd been bracing for a sensational, crowd-pleasing yarn akin to her book's, found himself impressed by the seriousness of the presentation. First, Wheatman's poise was like that of an academic lecturer at ease before an audience. And while she did indeed touch on her own story, which began with the massacre of her family, and then described her "slavery" to the Mohave—ending with her rescue by the 9th Cavalry of buffalo soldiers—her overarching subject was no less than the history of the captive trade in North America. Consequently, he found himself absorbed. For instance, he had not been aware of the story of Hannah Duston of Massachusetts, a mother of nine who in 1697 was taken prisoner by the Abenaki only to slaughter her underestimating captors with a hatchet and return to her village with their scalps. Neither had he known that the Puritans put a price on each Indian scalp, nor that the Five Civilized Tribes of the southeast held thousands of black captives who followed them to the reservation. Finally, toward the end of her talk, her audience learned that, according to the Census of 1870, which counted Indians who had "renounced tribal rules," up to thirty percent of certain tribes were of mixed race.

Following her prepared speech, Miss Wheatman took questions from the audience. The majority were related to her life as a slave and her longing to go home. Only toward the end of the session did anyone question her facial marks. A woman rose from the assembly to ask if they "represent marriage, as some suggest, or do they signify acceptance to the tribe?"

At this, Ophelia Wheatman straightened herself in her high-necked collar. Without a trace of pique, she answered, "Neither conclusion is accurate. These are the marks of Mohave slavery, pure and simple." She seized the opportunity to end the lecture thus: "I'm pleased to announce that my publisher plans a third printing of the book. Until then, stocks are few. I urge you to purchase your copy today from Mr. Leary. We thank you." With that, she curtseyed to her audience and was rewarded with applause.

"Smooth," Renald observed for Kirkby's ears.

Meantime, Mr. Leary, patting his brow with a handkerchief, announced a five-minute break during which the crowd should form a signing line. He gestured to a table stacked with copies of *My Life Among the Apache and Mohave.*

Dr. Kirkby nudged Renald. "Want to meet her?"

As Miss Wheatman stepped from the dais with her host assisting feebly, Dr. Kirkby and Scott Renald made their way through the crowd. The doctor used his size to their advantage, pushing straight to the speaker, who, with Mr. Leary at her side, greeted Kirkby with a glowing smile before shifting her gaze tentatively to Renald.

Dr. Kirkby offered introductions all around.

"If I'm not mistaken," she said to Renald, "you are the famous captive hunter whose nephew is Chief Talking Moon. They say you're the best."

He removed his hat. "The Comanche owed me a debt, Miss Wheatman. I lost loved ones to them—two dead, one held like you. They let me trade on it again and again."

"I regret your losses, Mr. Renald," she replied. "However, recovering others must afford you some measure of consolation each and every time."

"Every time I brought home a rescue, it did help me, ma'am."

"It's a pity for me you weren't posted in Apache country. Maybe I wouldn't wear these marks."

From his little knowledge of the Mohave, he knew enough to guess that the exposed tattoo was just the beginning—or was it the end?—of a much more elaborate decoration covering her entire body. Ophelia Wheatman not only wore a high collar, he noticed, but long cuffs as well.

"Those marks …" he said, losing his self-restraint, "and yet, you maintain you weren't married."

Her cordial, high-cheeked expression collapsed. "I do, sir."

Instantly, Dr. Kirkby protested. "Mr. Renald, you go too far."

Was it the term "married" that she did not accept? After all, a native marriage was un-Christian, unrecognized. Renald continued in spite of himself. "The public wants good stories. Being married to a Mohave chief would've made a better one."

Dr. Kirkby gasped again. This time Mr. Leary butted in, indicating the growing line of customers. "I believe it's time …"

Ophelia Wheatman added firmly, "There's just so much the public can accept, Mr. Renald."

Convinced by her marks that she had indeed been married to a Mohave headman, Renald found himself believing the rumors that she'd left a daughter in the Indian camp. The former searcher in him couldn't resist digging for the truth. "By that, you mean the public wouldn't accept a child left behind …"

Dr. Kirkby flushed. Miss Wheatman downright blanched.

Collecting himself, the doctor demanded, "Mr. Renald, what on earth possesses you?" Kirkby turned to his former patient as she began to well up. "You are expected at the signing desk, Ophelia."

But Ophelia Wheatman stood her ground against Renald. "Surely you are not suggesting I go back to the Indians."

"No, ma'am."

Her eyelids fluttered, spilling tears. "Then you must be implying I should make efforts to extract a child from her world and force her into mine."

"I am," he said. "But, then, you don't have a child, do you, Miss Wheatman?"

She swallowed before replying. "Would clothing her in dresses and sitting her at table be fair?"

"It's not about fair," he said, "it's about the future. If you had a girl, she'd be no more than what, six years old?"

Ophelia Wheatman revealed nothing. That said something.

"Talking Moon's son was six years old when he came in," he said. "It still works at that age. I know."

She pursed her lips, then mustered a curt, "Goodnight, Mr. Renald."

Renald turned away thinking about that black girl in the tintype who nobody was looking for. If the government's current talks with the allied Apache chiefs failed, Emma Neely wouldn't be wearing dresses again anytime soon.

Chapter Six

Pioneer's Rest was Fort Worth's oldest cemetery, dating back to Major Ripley Allen Arnold's orders in 1849 to establish a permanent camp "at or near the confluence of the West Fork and the Clear Fork of the Trinity River." A veteran of the Mexican War who'd served with Scott Renald, Major Arnold inauspiciously named Camp Worth for their late commander, dead of cholera in San Antonio. Within a year, the major would bury two of his daughters and 11 of his 42 soldiers there. In 1853, Arnold joined them, shot dead by a fellow officer in questionable circumstances.

The crowded burial grounds lay a mile from the city grid. A wrought iron entry sign arced above the gates, which Scott Renald presently parted with a groan of metal. Though a regular visitor, he'd never noticed the misplaced apostrophe in the sign under which he now passed: *Pioneer's Rest*. Not one, but 500 graves had been dug in the cemetery's short existence. His wife's was one of them.

For a long time, he didn't know whose remains were buried down there—hers or his sister's. The Comanche raid on their homestead while he was on patrol had resulted in a fire that left only one skeleton in the ashes. Unable to mourn for a specific loved one, and plagued by the thought that one of the women was still alive—somewhere—for three decades he searched the southern plains for the truth, finally discovering that his sister had died the wife of a Comanche chief. Until then, the headstone had simply read *Renald,* allowing for a given name when there was one to give it.

Today, he laid a bouquet before the slab of marble that bore his wife's name and, with its rounded shoulders, doubled for her in his imagination. Renald squared his own shoulders and drummed the brim of his hat.

"Dolly?" He whispered her name as if he might actually rouse her. "To start with, you're probably wondering why I'm out here on a weekday ..." He absorbed the tranquil scene before him, glistening from the morning dew. "This spring air sure recalls our last county dance, doesn't it? Such a small affair back then. Remember what you wore to it? A red and white checkered dress. You were just beginning to show ..." Thumbing his heaving chest, he said, "I felt so damned lucky you'd come out here for me. Yours wasn't only a love. It was a faith—in me. We were building something." Troubled by the memory that followed, he regarded the rows of tombstones around him. "A familiar story in here, I'm afraid."

He shifted his weight, and therefore the burden on his hips and knees. Then, as if responding to her, he said, "Yep, I'm a talkative one today. Funny how a resting place can turn even a quiet man into a talker."

From the north came two distant whistle blasts from a locomotive, as if signaling him to spit it out.

Renald choked up at first. "A few weeks ago," he continued, "I received a visit from Black Jack Davidson and his top sergeant, a Negro fella named Chance. The short of it is, Davidson wants me to ride out for a white warrior—a teenager once taken by the Apache who took a scalp down in Mason County. Of course, I turned them down flat, but Chance left me with this—" He pulled the tintype from his breast pocket. "It's a Negro girl, age four, taken from Chadbourne. Her name is Emma." Tapping it, he added, "Neely—Emma Neely. The name didn't mean anything to me at first. But then I got to thinking, wasn't it a sergeant name of Neely who once shot an Apache off my back?"

He levelled his gaze at the tombstone.

"Most white captives are ransomed back. That's why they're taken in the first place. But a little black girl gone missing? Nobody gets orders to ride out for her. Before long, she's doing menial labor, and if she's lucky some lonely or barren squaw forms an attachment to her. To my mind, this Emma is the one needing rescue—not that scalping German—but nobody's making a fuss about her. What's her mother supposed to do?" He rubbed his scalp through thick, silvery hair. "Knowing Tops, he's probably put hopes in that woman's head about me—why, she might even be praying for my help this very minute. That doesn't sit well, not with my doing nothing about it. Here I am, situated in Fort Worth to be near *you*, to be near young Jimmy, to raise my horses—to *rest*. And yet …"

For a moment, he let his eyes close. Then, "I haven't been sleeping well knowing that Neely girl is out there somewhere, without a chance." He paused. "A chance?"

Renald regarded the photo thoughtfully before slipping it back in his pocket. "Maybe there's something to that, for those who believe in divine providence. Should *I*, Dolly— *believe in providence?*" He dug his heel in the dirt, clutching his hat, belatedly aware of the sweet call and response of a pair of yellow-breasted chats above. Continuing, he said, "First Emma's folks are visited by Tops Chance, and now in answer to their prayers I'm actually pondering it. Thing is, I haven't a clue where to look for her. It's not even known which tribe took her. By now she could be traded into New Mexico, Nevada, Colorado. But I do have a fair idea where I'll find *him,* that white warrior. Davidson wired Friday about a hostile sanctuary in Saline Valley." Shifting his weight yet again, he said, "The boy's name is Karl—or was. He's the one I took that arrow for."

Renald shrugged and fitted his hat back on. "So, Dolly, what shall I do about all this?"

He lingered for a while in the cool draft through the pines— waiting for some kind of sign? At last he stepped behind the tombstone, placing his gloved hands affectionately on its smooth, dewy shoulders and leaning forward to whisper as if in Dolly's ear. "What if I put it in God's hands and just ride out?" he asked.

With that—with his answer—he gave the cold stone a peck, and departed.

* * *

He didn't leave Fort Worth right away. Having come to a decision of sorts, he felt inclined to first call on Karl's mother. The last time he'd seen Trude Hermann, his arm was in a sling. She and Gunter, overcome with joy at Freddie's return and still hopeful about Karl, brought an oversized and overstuffed gift basket to Renald at the post. To this day he remembered the handmade sausages, the bottles of berry and fruit liqueurs, and the "bee sting" cakes—caramelized, crisp, and custard-filled.

Yet, despite the Hermanns' show of gratitude and well wishes, when his injury was mended Renald had chosen to end his career on the mixed success of Freddie's rescue. Karl would remain unredeemed.

As he rode down Main Street, it seemed as if every tenth person saluted or otherwise acknowledged him. Unlike other cattle towns that had sprung up in recent years—only to die as the beef trails changed—Fort Worth was built to last. Once marked on a map as "Where the West begins," today that line might be drawn at the border of New Mexico Territory, a distance of some 300 miles. Thus Fort Worth, with its planned city grid and stone public buildings, was a symbol of a country no longer in dispute. Like others who'd lost loved ones in the conquering, Renald felt a founder's pride in its workings, its busyness, its enduring legacy.

He paid a courtesy call on the post office operator before heading upstairs. Then, hat in hand, he rapped on Mrs. Hermann's door.

A clack of heels promptly arose behind it. The door cracked open to reveal a pretty but drawn and suspicious face with brown eyes that suddenly brightened.

"Why, Mr. Renald!" She swung the door open and stepped into the gap. The faded floral print housedress she wore resembled an old dishrag.

He doffed his hat. "Hope you don't mind my stopping by unannounced, ma'am."

Her smile breathed some life back into her pallid cheeks. "Your shoulder is better?" She spoke with a heavy accent.

He rolled it, replying in the affirmative. Then, anglicizing her surname in pronunciation, he asked, "Might we have a word, Mrs. Hermann?"

Holding the door close, she answered, "Naturally you are welcome, Mr. Renald. However, I am afraid our home is not suitable for receiving guests. Perhaps we meet us at Martha's across the street?"

"Sure you want to have this conversation in public?"

Her cheeks paled again. "Karl is … is? …"

"Oh, he's all right far as I know."

Chin up, she said, "Then we meet us at Martha's."

"I'll be waiting, ma'am." He turned and headed back downstairs.

Ten minutes later she entered the brightly lit Martha's Restaurant-Saloon. She'd changed to a forest green dress, let down her reddish-brown hair, and thrown on some makeup. She drew plenty of attention from the mostly male customers.

Renald sat nursing a cup of coffee at the farthest of four round tables opposite the bar counter, where a few men were seated with their backs to him. From behind the wooden counter, the proprietress greeted Trude Hermann with a smile of familiarity.

Renald hastened to his feet as Mrs. Hermann came over. "What can I get you?"

Taking a seat, she answered, "Martha shall bring me tea."

He sat down opposite her. "Slice o' pie? She claims she's quite a baker."

"Her *apfel* pie Freddie loves. You must try it."

"I should," he said, "but I won't. How about a glass of sherry?"

"At nine-thirty in the morning, Mr. Renald?"

"Well, you're German. And the topic is heavy."

She shook her head, smiling politely.

"How is Freddie?" he asked.

"*Gut*—at school," she responded. Then, "Sometimes with his friends he pretends he is *you* rescuing them, finding Karl."

"Does he know about Karl, what he's done?"

A frown. She clasped her hands together on the table between them, turning her knuckles white. "No," she replied. She blinked, her eyes rosy. "For you I am waiting weeks, Mr. Renald."

He did not have a response ready.

"You know I am so grateful to you for finding Freddie. But as much as I love him, he is a constant reminder of my son who is lost." She choked back tears. "Can you imagine, Mr. Renald?"

He plucked his napkin from the table and offered it to her. She buried her face in it. On top of grief and worry, he thought, she must be feeling an awful lot of shame these days.

Recovering at last, she forced herself to speak. "Colonel Davidson tells me you have a beautiful ranch."

"A beautiful *little* ranch. You're welcome to visit anytime," he responded. "Forgive my bluntness, Mrs. Hermann, but didn't the colonel tell you I turned him down?"

Patting her cheeks with the linen, she replied, "What else can I do other than hope?"

At first, he did not reply. Hope was all she could have, unresolved loss being the worst kind. But then, to her instant look of surprise, he said, "There's a Negro mother who's hoping and praying too. I reckon Sergeant Chance left that out."

She nodded, guardedly.

"A little girl was taken from the Chadbourne area."

Squeezing her eyes shut, she replied, "When will it stop?"

The aproned proprietress stepped in with the pot of tea. Pouring, she met Renald's gaze. "So you're the man who found Freddie—and so many others."

"Mr. Renald," Mrs. Hermann clarified.

Martha eased back, hand on hip. "Most everybody around here knows Scott Renald on sight." She appraised him up and down. "You still look mighty Army. Hell, you still look *mighty*. Honored to make your acquaintance."

With that, Martha left them alone, but not before she gave the widow a suggestive lift of the eyebrow.

Mrs. Hermann's chest rose and fell. "Is your visit a sign you have changed your mind, Mr. Renald?"

That he'd just been mulling the matter over with his deceased wife went unmentioned. He took a contemplative sip of coffee and let his gaze return to Mrs. Hermann's tense, intertwined fingers. She was still wearing her wedding ring. As was he.

"Did you know that Davidson sent three men after Karl? An agent and two scouts. They … disappeared."

She said nothing. Was the outcome too grave to acknowledge?

"Yet he still feels he owes you your son," he continued. "And now he thinks he knows where he is."

"Yes?" Hope had returned to those brown eyes.

"Scouts report a large Indian camp at the Kickapoo Springs. Mason is striking distance from there."

"Mr. Renald, I have no right to ask you …"

"You don't have to," he said, gathering himself. "Traveling on a commission to trade is the safest way into Indian country. To be honest, I've been fretting about that Negro girl."

Mrs. Hermann drew back, aghast. "You think she is more deserving than *mein Sohn*?"

"Karl isn't a captive anymore. But the commission is for him, so I've decided to accept it …"

This provoked fresh tears.

"I'll be keeping an eye out for the girl as well," he said. "Unlikely I can return with both. If I come across her first …"

The men at the bar, chins jutting over shoulders, were obviously pinned to every word, while Martha was polishing glasses as if all was regular.

"It is selfish from me," Mrs. Hermann admitted, "but I want my son." Now, in a voice trembling with emotion, she added, "Unless he will hang."

Renald cocked his head. "If I were you, I wouldn't worry about that. The law shrugs off such cases."

After a sniffling pause, she asked, "Why do you think he did it?—if he did it."

Renald imagined Karl Hermann bending over the body of his settler victim, cutting him from ear to ear, and then carving out and tearing off his scalp. "Karl's Apache now, simple as that," he answered. "Question is, why'd he do it back in Mason?"

"Are you asking me, Mr. Renald?"

"He knows Loyal Valley," he went on, "where to go, who to steal from, and how to get out. He's what, sixteen today? Maybe it was his first raid. Maybe with it he had something to prove—and something to say to us too."

"To say?"

"Maybe one of the things that kept him alive in captivity, and eventually made him a warrior, was a grudge—against us for forgetting him. The way he saw it, anyway."

"I did not forget him." Her eyes, still red and puffy, had dried.

He didn't need to remind her that even her husband had eventually ended his search. She said nothing more, perhaps remembering that Gunter never forgave himself for sending those boys out scarecrowing that day.

Renald got to his feet, reaching for his wallet with one hand and slapping his hat on with the other. "If Karl's at the Kickapoo, it'll be a while."

He eased her chair out, and she rose. "And if she is there too?" Her voice, wary now, had regained its timber. "The black girl?"

"The girl's father fought with us in that raid. He saved my life before I had the chance to rescue Freddie. I hope you understand."

"I see. And what is her name? That girl?"

He told her.

Mrs. Hermann nodded. "She will be in my prayers as well."

Part II
Toward Ben Ficklin

Chapter Eight

When Scott Renald looked back on his career as a Plains trooper and, later, as a civilian scout, his thoughts were often dominated by visceral memories of the heat, the dust, and the thirst endured on his desert rides. Today, by contrast, in spring, the climate welcomed rather than opposed him, and as he rode with his captive deeper into hostile terrain he found himself marveling at the wildflowers blanketing the rolling prairie around him—fiery oranges and reds, splashes of mustard and white, regal violet blues, all peppered by jet black daisies. At a certain age, a man starts noticing the flowers.

From the years he'd operated out of present-day Fort Concho, he remembered the approximate location of the Kickapoo Springs. But the Lipan could be encamped anywhere along the streams that ran from them. Due to the amount of loose sediment in the Kickapoo, whose waters remained brown all year, the army sourced its fresh water further west at the Pecos Springs. Doubtless, the Kickapoo's undesirability accounted for the Indians having made a lasting camp there, right under Fort Concho's nose.

Renald and Chivatá were spotted by lookouts about a mile from the spring's south-flowing offshoot. A few riders approached atop painted mounts and Renald felt the old danger-tingles charging his spine. But these men didn't react immediately to the sight of one of their own bound at the wrists. After all, Chivatá's capture and return was proof of her victor's charitableness. They must have admired the man who could best the legendary female pair of Nalen and Chivatá.

Without unnecessary drama, the party reined to a stop before them. Each of the young men seemed to consider the implications of the situation. Finally, one of them took the lead, attempting to speak with Chivatá.

She averted her gaze, lips pursed, and gave him the same cold shoulder she'd previously afforded Renald. That her silence reflected a wounded pride was evident in the warrior's reaction. He dismissed her with a comprehending nod and addressed Renald directly.

"Talk Apache? *Habla español?*"

Renald's grasp of Spanish was sufficient to know he'd been addressed with respect. "Wish I did," he answered. "*Jefe*—I want to see your *jefe.*"

Again, the warrior attempted to communicate with Chivatá, but she simply lowered her chin. Giving up, he pointed at the white man's weapons—first at his sidearm, then at his long gun in its slip. "No guns," he said.

"No guns? No problem!" Renald pulled his saddle gun and extended it stock first toward the brave. A second warrior heeled his mount forward and opened a hand. Renald withdrew his pistol and finger-spun it to him. "Got the women's guns packed …" He indicated his saddle bags.

"Bueno," replied the lead warrior. *"Ahora ..."* He regarded Chivatá's shackles and mimed the turning of a key.

Renald shook his head. "First, your chief."

The men just behind the lead brave awaited his reaction. After scrutinizing Renald a little longer, he reined his pony around.

The prairie was fairly scattered with trees, and lush growth marked the springs. From a distance, the encampment within was invisible. As they drew nearer, however, tepee tips revealed themselves within the acacias and ash trees. A little closer and Renald detected movement in there. He could also smell the livestock. When their party reached the camp perimeter, the lead warrior cast a look back at Renald as if to say, "Here we go ..." He then offered a shrill halloo to the air, indicating possession of a prisoner. It was echoed back by someone inside the timber. With that, the men surrounding Renald and Chivatá all signaled their mounts forward and rode together into the camp's alternating patches of shadows and light.

Meeting them was another group of mounted men. One exchanged words with the warrior into whose charge Renald had fallen, and then hauled his mount around and rode back into camp.

The village projected a somber mood, insufficiently explained by the shackled Chivatá, though the sight of her as a white man's prisoner drew some gawkers. Rather, it was a gloominess that Renald had the feeling of entering into. Something had happened here. He could see it in the sullen faces of the men greeting their party, and in the women and children standing rigidly outside their abodes. Absent was the cheerful mix of activity indicative of an Indian camp at the height of morning. Where were the rollicking young ones? Or the circles of women doing handiworks or skinning game? Where were the men making arrows or carousing, or merely reclining after a strenuous hunt? True, Renald had only just entered the village, but in his experience a common disposition, whether subdued or festive, was shared throughout an entire camp.

Just what had transpired here?

He witnessed more of the same as he and Chivatá were led toward the village center. At last they stopped at a large tepee decorated with a blood painting of a buffalo hunt, its conical shape lending an illusion of movement to this scene. As he was led clockwise to the door flap, Renald observed how the hunt ended with a heap of buffalo at the bottom of a ravine. Outside the tepee door was a small campfire, a sight so common before a headman's lodge that, to Renald, it did not recall the Northern People engagement.

Seconds later, the guardian warrior who'd met their party minutes before emerged from behind the door flap. Next out was the headman, bedecked in a feathery headdress—a wiry elder with a scarred face and a mauled ear. He was immediately taken aback at the sight of Chivatá, alone and bound. Renald was inclined to dismount out of respect, but nevertheless remained where he was. It was safer to be still. In any case, the old man barely heeded him, instead training a look of disappointment on his remaining woman warrior.

Scowling, he berated her in a voice that caused everyone to shudder. Then, thrusting a finger toward the ground between them, he seemed to order her down from her mount. A tense, wind-whistling moment followed before Chivatá, sucking in a breath, crossed her right leg over her saddle horn and slid off. The headman, still without acknowledging Renald, examined the wound in the woman's forehead, his thumb testing the dried gouge above her right eye. She winced.

Loudly, he scolded her—for what, Renald could reasonably guess. She'd recklessly broken the peace and picked a fight that led to Nalen's death and the loss of a horse. That her bester was now at their mercy was no matter. The old man stamped a moccasined foot throughout his tirade. Weathering his fury under a torrent of spittle, Chivatá avoided his eyes as much from shame as from respect.

Renald produced the key to her shackles from his pocket and diverted attention from her by waving it around. Then, feeling at liberty to, he dismounted and stepped to her side. After a distracted nod from the headman, who was still red with fury, Chivatá extended her wrists while averting her gaze, chin raised with wounded pride. Renald unbound her and clipped the cuffs back onto his belt.

Collecting herself, she said, "Chief Tall Grass asks why he should not kill you." Her voice was husky and disdainful.

Renald didn't trust the translation. The fact that he'd delivered her alive must have counted for something. Surely it had spared him thus far. He held out his left hand in a fist and capped it with his right. "Peace," he said.

At this Tall Grass spat, then cursed.

Chivatá continued. "Chief says you give the Comanche sign of peace. You Comanche?"

"By association," he answered. "My nephew is Chief Talking Moon."

The headman's eyes flared, then softened. He spoke, and Chivatá translated. "You are known to me—the white man who convinced Talking Moon to surrender."

"That's what they say," Renald answered.

"And now you are here to convince *me* to surrender?"

"I wish to request your help."

Tall Grass scoffed. "That you are the uncle of Talking Moon does not impress me."

"Frankly, Talking Moon doesn't impress me much either," said Renald.

The headman's eyes shone in fraternity before he replied, "But with his father—Chief Iron Mountain—I smoked many pipes. I shall hear your request."

So far, so good, thought Renald.

Practically anybody back home would consider it insanity to risk one's scalp for either a white warrior or a black girl, but he'd always come back from these missions in one piece and with a prize—if not with one captive, then another. Despite operating on a commission to find Karl, till now he'd been divided about the true object of this mission. Which child should he prioritize? The younger or the older? The black girl or the white boy? The boy would certainly fight him like a mountain cat. Renald fretted for an instant. To the headman, it must have seemed only a moment's hesitation. But it was a pause of significance. The tangle of emotion Renald felt at this choice was resolved by the memory of the heartbroken Trude Hermann—her loss, her sadness, her situation, and—yes— her quiet beauty.

He made his choice.

Against his better judgment, it would be the child who no longer needed him. "The brave who was Karl Hermann led a raid some weeks back, over in Mason," he explained. "At the time, nobody went after him. But now the yellow stripes know you're here." He concluded with a threat, albeit an empty one. "You know what that means."

Tall Grass erupted, with Chivatá translating rapidly. "While today our chiefs talk treaty? Chiefs of Red Clay People,

Green Mountain People, even Wild Goose People—all in Washington!"

"There is yet no peace," Renald answered. "Karl Hermann proved it when he took that scalp." Transferring his gaze to Chivatá, he added, "She proved it too."

The surrounding braves began to murmur among themselves. Tall Grass shot Chivatá another scolding look. "The bluecoats will not sacrifice talks over one scalp!" he protested.

"Won't they?" Renald held out his hand, palm up, as if Karl Hermann belonged there.

But Tall Grass muttered, "He is not here."

"Surely he's of your band. The Mescalero aren't of these parts."

"He ran off."

A lie? "When?"

"Earlier today."

Renald was dumbfounded. "Well, that's plumb timely!"

Their business apparently concluded, the headman ordered the return of the white man's weapons. The lead warrior heeled his horse over to Renald's and shoved the Winchester into its saddle slip. A second tribesman trotted forth and thrust the revolver down at him, butt first.

"*Gracías,*" said Renald, shoving the gun into its holster. He turned and dug into his saddle bags for the women's weapons. With a nod from her headman, Chivatá strapped her loaded gun-belt around her hips. Her knife dangled there, too, in its tasseled, beaded sheath—yet only for an instant. She quickly reached for it, causing all to flinch. But instead of using it on Renald, she turned it on herself, cutting through ribbon after ribbon of hair she bunched in her other hand. As her shavings lit up the camp-fire, she turned back and gave Renald her now familiar glower.

A moment passed, and Tall Grass told him, "This way …"

Instead of leading the white stranger eastward out of camp, the group turned west. Moving together through the shady sanctuary, they passed between lines of soaring tepees and domed wikiups. Here and there, with Chivatá's help, the headman offered commentary to his guest, be it about the significance of a particular tepee illustration, the long-ago feats of the illustrious elder who lived there, or merely how some of the children had gotten their names. All the while, the villagers ceased their activities and stared speechless after them. Many children were among those standing as if at attention outside the entrance flaps of their homes, some of the boys holding miniature bows and arrows at their waists, the girls bearing animal hides or knitting. Their parents wore grave looks beside them, as though inevitable change had finally come. This distinguished-looking visitor wasn't here for mere hides or trinkets. He wore a tied-down gun and his long, athletic stride carried him with a soldier's confidence. For a stranger and a white man, he was being treated with surprising importance. Why?

His sudden presence in the village would naturally lead people to worry. It was commonly known that, not too long ago, a paleface rode into Talking Moon's camp and the very next day the redoubtable Comanche leader surrendered. Little did these Apache villagers know that Renald was that very paleface.

For his part, Renald, smiling now and again at the children and tipping his hat at their parents, could see by the many men in camp that the practice of raiding had truly been suppressed. Tall Grass was a headman he could work with.

But if Karl had really fled, what good was Tall Grass?

Reaching the edge of camp where the stream was narrowest, the headman demanded a horse from his men. A young warrior offered him his, and Tall Grass climbed onto its back with surprising agility. The men all mounted their ponies, while the youth who had forfeited his own doubled up behind one of them. The party waded into the silty waters of the Kickapoo.

* * *

The temperate, breezy air held the stridulating music of a thousand crickets. Beyond lay a prairie dotted with trees, and a grassy eminence loomed a short distance northwest. Renald kept pace on Tall Grass' right, with Chivatá on her elder's left and the warriors further back.

From his mount, Tall Grass explained, "We took in the Northern People survivors. Among them were the boy you seek and the warrior who captured and adopted him. Their spirit man and his two sons came too."

Renald felt himself constrict. He had, after all, been visible to many in that Lipan camp. Yet no vengeful member of the Northern People had seemed to recognize him today. Did all white men look alike?

"The boy is called Endah," Chivatá translated. "White Boy."

"Imaginative," said Renald.

"Some days ago," Tall Grass continued, "Endah's father found him with our spirit man. He hurt the spirit man."

Was this incident responsible for the village's solemnity? A healer was inviolate. Physical harm done to such a figure would at the very least cause a communal trauma and, possibly, even a questioning of the band's medicine. Renald's arrival so soon afterward could only have intensified the feeling that disquieted spirits were turning everything on its head.

Tall Grass halted his animal and pointed toward the gentle rise beyond.

Renald strained his eyes. "Am I seeing two burial mounds up there?"

"Yesterday the spirit man took his revenge. He poisoned Endah's father."

Chivatá continued to translate, now with a tone of surprise and a look of shock. "Then, this morning, Endah took the spirit man's life."

Doubtless a cataclysmic event for the Lipan people. Silence followed Tall Grass' words as everyone present considered the consequences, not least of all Renald. You don't just pick shamans off a shelf, and besides that, the village had lost two men. "Under Apache law," he said, "isn't avenging a death justified?"

Tall Grass nodded. "The spirit man's sons now claim their own blood-right. They have gone after Endah."

"I must reach him first," said Renald instantly.

Tall Grass squinted his skepticism, his crow's feet forming deep cuts. "What makes you think Endah would listen to your call? He will fight. Great is his bow."

Renald scoffed. "He's just sixteen …"

Chivatá did not miss the opportunity. "And you are what? Sixty? Good luck."

Renald shrugged this off. Was Tall Grass going to help or not? Impatiently, he threatened, "If I don't ride back with him, the soldiers will ride out." It was a lie, but the Indians lied too—signing treaties only to break them after receiving food, supplies, livestock, money. "Deliver my horse to me and let me pass," he demanded.

The old man took a moment, lowering his gaze. Visibly, his disposition toward Renald seemed to change. Then, speaking through Chivatá, he said, "As you ride west, the threat you warn of could come from the east. The bluecoats might raid us anyway."

"Do you have a better idea?"

"Perhaps, then, you should ride ahead with knowledge that could spare us such a misfortune."

"I'm listening," said Renald, his curiosity piqued.

Referring to the nearest telegraph station, Tall Grass said, "The closest line that carries men's words is at Ben Ficklin, and it happens that Endah started in that direction." He straightened a long, bony finger westward. "Tell your chiefs that in the interests of peace, and because I do not support violent resistance, I offer them my own warning."

"Well, what is it?"

Tall Grass turned to Chivatá with a string of words. Renald made out only "Comanche" and "Sill" as Tall Grass swiped his hand dramatically from east to west. That was enough, though, for Renald to start connecting the dots. Meantime, the headman's pronouncement roused a look of belligerence in Chivatá's eyes. She protested in fiery words lost on Renald.

Dismissing her objections, Tall Grass addressed Renald again. Chivatá crossed her arms over her chest, refusing to translate. This set Tall Grass off, and he struck her shoulder with the back of his hand—only her shoulder for now.

Renald could feel the men's tension around him. Chivatá's skin tautened over her cheeks. She spoke through a petulant scowl. "It is said there will be a breakout from Fort Sill. Many warriors will cross the Llano and unite with Geronimo and Caballero."

She stopped there.

A Comanche breakout and the prospect of a greater Indian war, no less. Renald felt himself freeze. Might Talking Moon himself be behind it? As the former war leader's uncle, he couldn't help but wonder.

"Perhaps it is only talk," Tall Grass added with a shrug.

"Talk is enough for me. The army needs to know. *Ashagoteh!*" he said, possessing at least this much Apache. "Thanks!"

"Follow me, then, to where Endah's trail begins."

The three descended the grassy rise and trotted south, the village now hidden in the trees to their left. Behind them rode the warrior escort. After a few minutes, they stopped at an old buffalo trail, and Tall Grass pulled rein. "Here lie his tracks." He dismounted, and with Renald and Chivatá following suit, he pointed downward. Three sets of fresh horse tracks practically jumped out at them—Endah's and his pursuers, if the chief was reliable. With his moccasin boot, Tall Grass wiped smooth a patch of dirt. Then, after barking a demand, he took an arrow feathers-first from the quiver of one of his braves. With the arrowhead, he sketched a map on the ground: first, an almost straight north-south line that could represent a boundary, or a river. Next, a foot to its left, he kicked up a pile of dirt. Finally, with his buckskin heel, he smudged a single point on the line.

Indicating this last mark, he said, "The town of Ben Ficklin on what you call the South Concho River. Here you can alert the army. If Endah makes it that far, he will avoid the town and cross the river upstream."

Renald noted the headman's cracked, drawn visage under his headdress. "And go where?" he asked him.

"The Apache Mountains. Three days' ride."

Though Renald had never seen the so-called Apache Mountains, he responded, "That place must be crawling with

Mescalero and Chiricahua. They'd conclude he's a Lipan on the run." With the toe of his boot he drew an arcing route north from the river. "If I was him, I'd head into Comanche country. No risk of being held for you—or returned."

Chivatá translated and Tall Grass nodded, a glint in his eye. "You could be right. Endah traded with them last week."

"Traded? For what?"

The headman observed him with surprise. "*For a horse.* And not a very good one."

Only later would Renald realize his error. Instead of asking what Endah had traded for, he should have asked what he'd held for trade.

With that, Tall Grass turned his focus to Chivatá, making some demand of her. She argued back forcefully, looking him straight in the eye as if his equal. At last, Tall Grass ended her protest with a piercing cry that must've sent chills up even the horses' spines. Then, after pausing to glare at her—and surely to catch his breath too—he launched into a final diatribe that concluded with him jutting his chin toward Renald.

Chastened, Chivatá communicated his message in a grudging tone. "To catch up with Endah, you need a good tracker. Someone who speaks English, and who can convince his pursuers to stand down. You have all three qualities in Chivatá."

Offering a conciliatory smile, Renald said, "I'd be glad to have your company." Then, gesturing toward the weapons on her hip, he added, "Provided you don't pull one of those on me."

Her blazing eyes told him she might.

Tall Grass prodded her to say more. With a grimace, she conceded, "All of us have blood on our hands. This white man was only defending himself. Chivatá is strong enough to acknowledge her fault, and to pay for it."

Renald leaned in to her. "In the army, we call this eating your own shit. I've had to eat a fair share of my own."

With time growing ever more precious, Renald pivoted on his heel toward his mount. When nobody attempted to stop him, he climbed into the saddle. Hand on chest, he offered Tall Grass his thanks, adding, "May your people enjoy good hunting this season."

The sentiment was nice, but for Renald the feeling was mixed, his fingers having unintentionally tapped the cloaked image of Emma Neely in his shirt pocket—recalling his cruel choice.

Chapter Nine

Regarding Endah's intentions, Renald was convinced of only one thing—that he planned to disappear by crossing the South Concho so close to Ben Ficklin that any Apache pursuers dare not follow. If timed right, the fleeing youth could lessen the risk of discovery by fording it at night. From the far side, if he didn't continue westward toward the Apache Mountains, or arc southwest toward the Ghost Mountains, he would head north past Fort Concho and toward the alkaline flats and mazelike canyons of the Llano Estacado, still a refuge for renegade bands of Comanche and Kiowa.

As the miles and hours passed, Renald let Chivatá do her work without interference, impressed by how she could spot—from her saddle, let alone on foot—a torn spider's web, a cracked twig, or a scattering of pemmican crumbs. Though she remained all but silent throughout their ride, Chivatá nevertheless led with her expertise, occasionally whispering, "This way …" or "Here …" before swinging up onto her pony. For him, relying on an expert tracker, and one better than himself, was an unusual luxury and an invitation for his mind to drift.

Again, Renald found himself questioning the logic, even the validity of his pursuit of the white warrior. Endah's fleeing *west* was the act of an Apache running from his own people, not of a white boy breaking free at last. But Karl need no longer feel abandoned by his true family, and for his mother's sake he should be presented with a choice. Finally, whatever guilt Renald had felt about prioritizing Karl over Emma Neely was replaced by the imperative to reach the telegraph at Ben Ficklin. There was always a chance he might locate Emma on the return, since she could be anywhere.

And what about Renald's reluctant companion? He watched as Chivatá, leading a few steps ahead on her grey and white mount, swayed appealingly from side to side in her saddle with her pony's steps. Here was an Apache-born woman who from an early age, the story went, had grown up in Mexico with a Confederate command that had refused to surrender after Appomattox. What were the contributing circumstances? Unmistakably present in her Apache accent were traces of a southern lilt. In time, perhaps, Renald's curiosity would be satisfied.

* * *

Chivatá shook her head and rose from a crouch. When she didn't remount, Renald knew it was time to quit for the day. Dusk had decided that.

They were at the edge of a clearing that was as good a place as any to pitch camp in. Without remark, Renald stepped down from his saddle and started unfastening it. Chivatá followed his lead, shoulders hunched from fatigue. Maintaining such levels of concentration throughout the day exhausted anyone. At his age, just riding from sunrise to sundown was sufficient. If he were younger, he'd be resolving to stay up all night rather than risk getting his throat cut in slumber. After all, he had nearly as much to fear from Chivatá as from the others. But he wasn't young, and he accepted that he had to risk death tonight to face it fresh tomorrow.

They unrolled their bedding a few feet apart. The air was crisp again. Dropping his hat onto his rubber mat, he felt a sense of relief. For all his mental indiscipline on the trail, nothing bad had come of it in the form of a bullet or an arrowhead. He made a small cook fire while his companion washed up with canteen water at the side of the campsite. She rinsed and wrung out her headband, a kind normally worn by men, and hung it from a branch to dry.

When she sat down opposite Renald, her oval eyes looked big and round for an Indian's, her cheekbones pronounced and glowing in the firelight. Her eyes sparkled from the light cast by the licking flames, and on her brow was the wound Renald had given her, the scab mostly crumbled away.

He poured a cup of coffee and passed it across to her, then tapped his own forehead. "I'm sorry about that gash …"

She met his gaze with a cold, baffled look. "Why? I tried to kill you."

He swallowed. "You still can—try, I mean."

"Do not tempt me."

"I regret what happened to your friend too."

"Because we are forced to work together? I'm used to loss."

"We all are," he replied.

She acknowledged it with a sullen nod, her gaze lost in the flames.

He sipped from his cup. "When we catch up to your friends, it'll get complicated. Won't it?"

"You keep trying to get me to talk."

"Well, why the hell not? The trees don't, and I'd like it if you did."

After a sigh, she said, "For now I do what Tall Grass wishes. But make no mistake. I am not—how do you say?—*on your side*." Absently, she ran two fingers over her grazed brow.

"Shouldn't do that," he admonished. He stood up. Feeling the stiffness in his legs and the soreness in his bad hip, he staggered over to his saddle bags. He returned with a bottle of whiskey in one hand and a wad of cotton in the other. Kneeling beside her—with effort—he offered to clean the wound.

She relieved him of the whiskey bottle with an abrupt grab, extracted the cork with her teeth, and spit it out. Up went the bottle.

"Hey, that's medicine, not drink!" he protested. "How about a bit above the eye too?"

She downed another generous swig and thrust the bottle at him. He took it and trickled some on the chunk of cotton. "May I?"

Now, as he tipped her chin up, not only did he find himself feeling close to her, he wondered if she might be softening toward him. He pressed the cotton wedge gently to her skin, and with his fingers lingering on her cheek, he felt her facial muscles tense. She pushed his hand away, and he withdrew with equal haste.

"Thank you," she offered.

"Well!" he remarked with surprise. "Don't mention it." He returned to the cook fire, where the tins of embalmed beef sat warming. With a gloved hand he pulled one can away from the coals. He punched it open and offered it to her, its lid bent and a fork sticking out.

She didn't hesitate. Between chews, she said, "You cook well."

Well? He gave a laugh. "*Well,* you say—not *good?* Not even I talk that good. Helps a man fit in out here." He grabbed for his own food tin, deciding to probe for the reason behind her faint southern drawl. "I recognize a touch of Tennessee in your voice," he said affably.

She hesitated before replying. "I was never in Tennessee."

"No need," he said, pressing. "Tennessee could've come to you …"

Her response took him aback. "Did you know General Shelby?"

"Joe Shelby? Sure do. Served with him in Sterling Price's command in the Mexican War. But he's from Missouri."

Another pause. "We were with his army in Mexico, after the American war."

"I heard something about that. You and—?"

"My mother."

That made sense, considering her age. "Did you know they added a verse to the Confederate anthem about him? About Joe Shelby?"

"Anthem?"

"The song of the southern states. I reckon it's safe to quote it here." He looked left, then right, almost theatrically, before reciting: "*I won't be reconstructed/I'm better now than then/And for a Carpetbagger I do not give a damn/So it's forward to the frontier, soon as I can go/I'll fix me up a weapon and start for Mexico.*"

She nodded. "They sang it."

"I bet they did. Tell me about your mother—and how you wound up down there with Joe."

When she hesitated, he egged her on. "Those trees sure won't tell me," he said.

Chivatá stuck her fork in the tin. "My mother was a slave of the Lipan Apache, down in Mexico. A Wichita slave."

"I see," he replied with a tinge of sympathy. Only a handful of the Wichita tribe remained. "Was she traded to one of his men?"

"After my father died. She was still young."

He absorbed this. "But Shelby returned in '67, following Maximilian's fall. You didn't learn English this well—uh, this good—in just two years."

"Some of his men and their families stayed on in Veracruz, some married Mexicans. We stayed—had to." Her expression darkened. "When my mother died, he … kept me for himself." Her voice trailed off bitterly.

Renald responded, "I'm sorry."

"I was fifteen at the time."

He bowed his head, searching for words.

Then, clearly relishing a memory, she added, "When I was seventeen, I killed him. Care to know how?"

"I'd rather not," he answered. "I'm sorry you went through all that."

"Chief Tall Grass' band had returned to Texas. I found them."

"Let me get this straight. You reunited with the very band that enslaved your mother?"

"She was a slave at the start, yes."

Renald ran his fingers across the stubble on his jaw. "I figured it would be quite a story. And what about the future? What do you want out of life? Just to kill more palefaces?"

"I want my friend back."

He concentrated on the fire, as if he could find Nalen there among the ashes. Instead he saw her corpse lying face down on a wildflower-spangled prairie.

"I was out there meaning well," he replied at last.

"Were you? Is one life worth so many?"

He met her gaze. "That's never the choice at the start," he said. "A man is only thinking about the one he's after."

Chivatá gestured toward the whiskey bottle beside him. "You don't drink?"

"Used to …"

"We drink too much …"

"You mean, you Indians? Well, most everybody has a reason out here. I sure did. But you're the first woman I've ever seen pull a cork with her teeth."

"I drink like a man," she replied, "I ride like a man … I even—"

"Shoot like a man? Kill like a man?" He couldn't help himself.

Her lips turned down, harboring the unspoken thought.

"It strikes me funny," he continued, "that you ride a white man's saddle, you speak his tongue, but when you meet a paleface on the open prairie your first instinct is to attack him. Is that how you two acquired those saddles?"

"There is no … What is the word? Contra—"

"Contradiction?"

Firmly, she replied, "I meant to protect my village."

"From a lone white man?" He sat up, shaking his head.

"White man rides alone is a scout or an agent—or in you, *both*."

"Do you think the army's really ignorant of your encampment at the Kickapoo? What they do about it depends on the man in charge at Fort Concho. Officially it's Ben Grierson, a kind man overall. But he's gone east on a family matter. Captain Norton has taken charge there."

"Norton?" she asked.

"Tenth Troop, A Company."

Short of an order from General Sheridan, Renald was confident Grierson wouldn't deprive the Apache of their water source—but Captain Norton was another story.

"Norton was disciplined for cowardice some years ago," he continued. "He turned back on a scout up on the Llano. He led that raid on the Northern People in '74, and still commands as if he's got something to prove."

Besides that, Renald mused, Norton was said to be in foul spirits since his wife died.

"Anyway," he concluded, "the forts nearby all source their water from the Pecos Springs—farther out, but fresher."

"We take what we can get," she replied, her bitterness registering.

"Only *what* you get keeps getting smaller—I hear you. But take the Comanche, the Cheyenne, the Kiowa, the Arapaho, other tribes too—they share a big place we call Indian Territory. Nearly a third the size of Texas." He was trying to sell it, he realized, like it was an almshouse.

Her response was sharp. "Sheep farmers! They have Indian Territory like we have the Kickapoo Springs—only for now! Where are the Kickapoo people today? Down in Mexico!"

"Can we stay on topic?" he asked. "You tried to kill me without cause, thinking I was Army. Lone army man means somebody who wants to talk, nothing more."

She shot him a look. "Do not speak of it again."

"I'd rather speak about you."

Grimacing, she asked, "What sort of man risks his life for others, alone, in Indian country?"

"The kind who's lost his own loved ones—to people like you."

After a long, fixed gaze, she replied, "I choose now to sleep."

He nodded. "Good idea."

Chivatá rose with enviable agility. She turned, and went to the fringe of the campsite glow.

He gazed into the dark depths of his open tin. "Sweet dreams," he mumbled.

Chapter Ten

Situated on the opposite bank of the South Concho River, the town of Ben Ficklin would be destroyed by flood on November 24, 1882, five years hence, and only Doc Thorndyke of those townsfolk who figure here would survive it. But today it was a boom town and the gateway to still-wild western Texas. While it didn't have the natural advantages of its raucous rival to the north, Saint Angela—built across from Fort Concho at the confluence of the North, Middle, and South Concho Rivers— Ben Ficklin was the Tom Green county seat and a place of comparative moderation. Its quietude notwithstanding, the town saw its share of itinerant hidesmen and cowboys, one as thirsty as the next.

At this late hour mid-week, the Wayward Saloon on Main Street was host to but a dozen or so customers—the usual cow punchers and locals playing cards or chewing the fat at tables strewn between the parlor doors and bar. Huddled at the counter was a trio of hydrating skinners. Merrily eastbound with a Murphy wagon and a buckboard heaped with skins, these hidesmen were uncharacteristically tidy for their sort.

"Spent the whole day in style!" explained the mustachioed Roy Danish, wearing trapper's skins, to a jowly and somewhat stooped barkeep. "We even got usselves shaved and bathed."

"But not laid," grunted one of his younger companions. Bo was a lanky, lightly bearded man in a freshly pressed shirt and bright red braces.

The barkeep leaned in. "You can get that *galore* upriver in Saint Angela …"

"Don't we know it," Danish grumbled. "But this time our trail took us this-a-ways." Then, teasingly toward one of his partners, he added, "Good thing we stopped off too! My buddy Bo here just picked up some fancy duds up the street."

He twanged Bo's suspenders, eliciting an "*Ow!*" and a look of protest from his partner.

"We even got usselves two rooms at the hotel," Danish finished.

"Well, glad to have you in Ben Ficklin!" replied the barkeep. "Come the weekend, we see a lot of business from Saint Angela. When it gets rowdy up there, the more proper elements retire down here."

"Right civilized town you got," Danish agreed.

"Not what you'd expect from the farthest-west town in Texas," said the third hunter, a clean-shaven, chaw-cheeked, curly-haired redhead called Reddy.

"And where does your journey take you?" the barman inquired.

Danish answered. "First to Fort Worth for the Texas & Pacific. Finally, to St. Joseph, Missouri, for the Skinners' Rendezvous—you done leave there empty-rigged every time. Best prices, too, for raw hides. Sure beats them cutthroats in Rath City."

"That right? I heard demand is down."

"You heard right," Danish conceded. "Tastes are a-changing in Europe. But supply's down as well. Over-trapping, over-hunting …"

"You fellas free hunters? Or d'ya belong to a brigade from one of them big outfits?"

The men chortled. Shaking his head, Reddy replied, "You're outta date, mister. Outfits like American Fur and Rocky Mountain Fur is all closed down. Men like usselves is looking for work as scouts, wagon train foremen, cow punchers."

"So what's your secret?" asked the barkeep. "Keen noses for the rare herd?"

Danish tapped his temple. "A keen mind, more like. *Mine.*"

The hunters shared another laugh. But Danish meant it. "Way I reckoned, the Apache wouldn't stir things up during them negotiations in Washington. That gave us a free pass."

"I dunno," said the barkeep, wiping down the counter. "Man lost his scalp last month as far in as Mason. Maybe you just got lucky."

Bo thumb-hooked his suspenders, and spoke up. "We didn't see as much as a lone injun!"

Sagely, Reddy offered, "Injun gets seen is'n injun wants to get seen."

Danish grunted before draining his glass. "We come back with our scalps and with hides is all I can say—is all I *care.*" He gestured toward the seated cowpokes. "Come next spring, I'll be looking for that sorta work. Gotta change with the times." Then, to his friends, "Take Cole Hawker, for instance. He put his Sharps away and got hisself a spread outside Fort Worth, and one o' them army beef contracts."

"Married a white squaw and took her son as his own," Bo added. "Who woulda thought Hawk could get hitched?"

"Not me," said Danish. "Or that he'd marry into money! That's the ex-governor's niece you're calling a white squaw. Why, you know what we should do, boys? See about working his stock! I oughta call on him in Fort Worth." He reached into his buckskin jacket for his wallet. "Well, time to settle up. Sam's all by his lonesome." Then, to the bartender, "We got a fellow hunter indisposed back at the hotel."

"That'll be five bits," said the barkeep. "Hope it's nothing serious. Doc Thorndyke is a neighbor of mine. I'll send him over first thing."

"Thanking you kindly for that." Danish flashed a smile and turned to his companions. Grasping the bar's edge with both hands, he said, "Looks like come morning, my so-called friends is abandoning me!"

"Aw, don't put it like that, Roy," said Bo. "Sam can't ride, and two nights in a hotel with our animals in livery is just too much."

Reddy nodded, and then aimed at the spittoon. *Clang.*

"Sure!" replied Danish, wise to their true intentions. "I don't blame you. If there ain't a woman in your bed, what's the point renting one? You go get your money's worth in Fort Worth!"

The men grinned. "Don't tell the wives," Reddy joked.

After sharing a final chortle, Danish tipped his hat to the barkeep. "I expect I'll be seeing you again tomorrow," he said. "We's obliged for sending that doc over."

"Don't mention it," replied the barkeep. "I hope your friend gets better quick."

Chapter Eleven

A soft easterly breeze tingled Renald's cheeks. It carried the sounds of a woman's muted chanting. When he became conscious of it, he shot upright in his blanket. Blinking his eyes clear, he found Chivatá's bedroll empty.

Then, peering beyond it toward a crescent of violet-tinged timber catching the faintest traces of dawn light, he discovered his companion. She was standing in a pool of moonlight, her silvery back to him. Facing north, she cut the air three times with her right hand, reciting in an Indian tongue he didn't recognize, but it didn't sound like Apache lingo. She turned to the east and cut the air thrice more, still chanting. She turned on her heels toward Renald and, noticing him watching, chopped the air between them. More chanting, and then she bent down and laid her palms in a patch of wiry turf, then brought up handfuls of torn grass and dispersed them into the air. At last, she rose to her feet, extending both arms toward the sky, palms out, chanting, *"Kinnikasus, Kinnikasus, Kinnikasus!"*

Renald threw off his cover. Grunting at his body's stiffness, he holstered his revolver. He'd slept gripping it to his chest, his boots on. But now, as his eyes shot left and right with caution, he became aware of his need to empty his bladder before carrying out his tasks. He looked about in frustration. For safety's sake, he always relieved himself in camp, but with a woman present he abandoned caution and treaded stiffly, warily, into the shadowy thicket. The ground crunched under his step. Here the starlight barely penetrated, but as he exposed himself in the darkness, he felt downright lamp-lighted.

He kept one hand on his gun butt.

* * *

While Chivatá packed up, he built a fire and cooked some coffee. Cheerful birdsong arose with the glow of false dawn. He warmed his hands over the fire before slipping on his gloves and stamping the chill from his feet. The kettle began to rattle. Steam issued. With a quick movement, he set it aside. *No time to eat now*, he was thinking, *not with sunup imminent*. Salt beef and hardtack on the trail would do. He poured a cup and held it out to catch Chivatá's attention. She finished strapping her bedroll behind her saddle and joined him, accepting the steaming cup with a surprisingly appreciative upturn of the lips. Her eyes shone brightly between long-lashed blinks. A fine-looking woman, he thought. Undeniable. Distracting. They sat down on opposite sides of the campfire and sipped from their cups. Thinking ahead to a quick departure, Renald set the grill aside to cool.

He swirled his coffee, bothered. "Your friends could be watching," he said in a voice that sounded stiff even to himself.

"The brothers would make contact with me," she responded.

He lowered his cup, scrutinizing her. "Have they?"

"No."

He attempted to see through the darkness behind her. "Just what are we up against?"

"The first son of the spirit man is called Burnt Face," she offered. "He is strong."

Renald repeated the name as a question.

"In the raid on the Northern People, a paleface threw him in the fire."

Renald swallowed and changed the subject. "How's your head? More whiskey?"

"No, thank you."

Her politeness registered. But how would she treat him when her loyalties were tested? "Those brothers," he continued. "If you don't convince them to stand down, I'll have to draw on them."

"They will kill you unless I stand between."

Renald knew better than to inquire if she would really intervene—because he had to assume she would not. But something else was on his mind. Unable to restrain himself, he asked, "How bad are they?—those face scars the medicine man's son carries?"

She looked startled, as if wondering why he should care about the one called Burnt Face. *When she discovers I did it,* thought Renald, *I'll have to draw on her like lightning.*

Chivatá's features flickered in the firelight. She lowered her cup. "Burnt Face is hard to look at," she said. "There is a place in the mountains where the outcasts go. He went there for a while."

Renald had heard tell of a sanctuary deep in the Apache Mountains for those born with birth defects, and others who'd lost a limb or an appendage for crimes or indiscretions.

"There he could live among those who do not stare," she said. "But he is too proud. Too proud to stay in camp, then too proud to stay away from it."

"Soon he won't need to be ashamed of his looks. Not if I have to face him."

"You are too sure of yourself."

"Am I?" His voice thickened. "Which side will *you* take? Each one has a blood-right. But Karl was born white, and he killed the medicine man. Will your loyalty to Tall Grass hold up?" Then he saw it—or thought he did. "Ah, but you're the daughter of a Wichita slave! Why should you care?"

Her chest rose. "Endah avenged the greater of two loves, each Apache. Like me, he is of two spirits. The healer looked upon him, and Endah let him."

Unmoved—and uncomprehending—Renald pressed on. "Background is not my concern. What matters is catching Karl and clearing anything in my path to do it. You included. Don't let it come to that."

Chivatá shot him a pitying look. "Perhaps *you* are why Endah is running west."

"*Me?*"

"In your world, he could not be understood. Not for what he truly is."

Shaking his head as if to unburden himself of comprehending it, he answered, "One thing's sure—he's a confused kid. But there's a head-doc in Fort Worth says he can fix anybody."

Her eyes narrowed. "Just who needs the fixing?"

Puzzled, he replied, "I don't understand."

"You sure don't!" she scoffed.

The break of dawn interrupted their back and forth.

As if following some established ritual, starting with sensing each other's next movement, when the lavenders of sunrise reached them, they rose simultaneously, tossed their coffee sludge to the side, and broke to see to their respective duties. Renald emptied the kettle and kicked dirt over the fire while Chivatá located the tracks of which she had seen only the faintest signs at sundown yesterday.

Renald brought up their mounts as Chivatá rose from a crouch. "We are closer than I thought," she said. "Us to them, them to him." She pointed at the ground. "Look. The quality of the sign is the same."

"How far to the river?"

"We will run into it soon."

"Seems like we're not going to make it in time."

Spotting equal concern in her eyes, he explained that they needed to throw caution to the wind, and just ride hard where possible through the scrub brush. They could make up an hour, maybe more. He was also conscious of the clock ticking on the imminent Fort Sill breakout, and the waiting telegraph at Ben Ficklin.

Such a clumsy approach to the river went against not only his training, it went against hers too. She shook her head.

He mounted up and spurred past her, taking the lead.

Chapter Twelve

At the hotel Sam wasn't any better, and while this youngest of Roy Danish's fellow hunters remained in bed, Danish saw the others down to the livery stable to collect their loaded wagon and buckboard. The day was pristine, the air biting at seven a.m. Shops were opening.

They found the bald, broad-shouldered proprietor in his office just inside the gate. "Morning, boys!" Ward O'Bannon rose from behind his desk to tower over all but Danish. His easy voice thundered. "So, how's Ben Ficklin been treating you? How's that infirm friend of yours?"

"Seems him and me gotta stay on another night," Danish answered. "As for the hospitality, we're real satisfied. Matter o' fact, I gotta return to the hotel for the doc's call."

"Thorndyke? Oh, he'll get him fixed up in no time."

Bo and Reddy lifted the canvas on the buckboard in the holding area and began counting their hides. The larger wagon, parked in a shadowy corner of the room, held an equal number of skins and all their equipment and necessities. Danish, smoothing his whiskers, ventured into the stables to greet his horse. Stamping her hooves in a stall she occupied with others, she was all too happy to see him. He rubbed her bobbing head, and she rewarded him with a snort in his face. Danish ambled back to O'Bannon's office to ask if they could leave their big rig with him a second night.

"Of course. And don't you fret. Ain't no crime in Ben Ficklin."

"Can't be too careful," said Danish. He gestured toward his partners completing their count. "No offense, but I advised my men here to check the inventory."

O'Bannon grinned. "Suit yourselves. How 'bout I boil you fellas some coffee before you hit the road?"

"Never can get enough," Reddy remarked through his morning chaw.

"I'll be heading back to the hotel now," said Danish. He embraced Bo, then Reddy, slapping them each on the back. Next, he asked O'Bannon if it was the flatboat landing that he'd seen from his hotel room.

"If you got a north view, yep—must be!" O'Bannon came out from behind his desk and glanced back and forth between Bo and Reddy. "Heading to Fort Worth, ain'tcha?" After receiving affirmative nods, he led them all outside. Squinting into the sunrise—the glare glinting off his bald pate—he pointed down Main Street. "You boys just cut left at the river on the military road, and you'll see the boat landing a piece ahead. The stage comes across there."

"Hope to see you at the station on Monday," Bo told Danish with a mischievous smile. "We'll wait fer ya overnight."

"You do that," Danish replied with a wink.

* * *

Roy Danish returned to the hotel. Upstairs, he hastened past the commode, conscious of Sam's discomfort in there, and once inside their double room, parted the curtains and opened the window for an unobstructed view of the river. The room welcomed the fresh air. With his hands planted on the window sill, he leaned out.

Moments later Sam joined him, blond and ashen-faced. He was clutching his gut under red long johns.

"How goes it?" asked Danish.

Sam shook his head. "One thing's sure—I'll never eat coon rare again."

"You oughta stay away from coon *entirely.* The doc'll be here any minute." Danish nodded toward the view. "Get yourself a look!" He changed places with Sam, who bent his knees to see an eastbound barge navigated by two men clutching long poles. It was clearly carrying a laden rig. Behind were two men on horseback wading into the river, each with a mule in tow.

"Damn shame," said Sam. "It's a long road to ride separate."

"If you're feeling good by tomorrow, we'll all meet up in Fort Worth on Monday."

Sam turned from the window. "I could eat. I guess that's a good sign. But I sure can't hold down no ham and eggs."

"Woman downstairs offered some rice at the doc's word."

Danish dropped into an armchair by the door while Sam collapsed onto the creaky bed.

"Them boys sure gonna have a hog-killin' time in Fort Worth," Sam predicted with an air of loss.

A knock rattled the door. Danish hastened to his feet and swung it open. Here was the physician in a dark grey suit, black hat, and holding the kit of his profession.

"C'mon in, Doc! Obliged for the early call."

The salt and pepper-bearded Thorndyke offered a hearty, "Good morning!" as he entered. With a nod of his whiskers he indicated Sam in bed. "I presume you're the patient."

"Got myself a case of the runs, Doc."

"Well, what'd you eat?"

"Coon … on the rare side."

"That'll do it! You hunt buffalo, don't you? Stick with that." Thorndyke opened his bag on the foot of the mattress. "Let's just eliminate some other possible causes, shall we? Pull those drawers down and lie on your back."

While the doctor saw to his patient, Danish returned to the window and watched Bo and Reddy completing the ford. They grounded the flatboat, unlashed and unblocked the rig, and rolled it onto the bank. He saw them tether the mules. Some money seemed to change hands, and the boatmen climbed back aboard and pushed off. The skinners threw canvas over the load.

"Any blood?" the doctor was asking.

"Frankly, I ain't looked," Sam answered.

"Well, look! You got some, stay another night and send somebody for me. Chances are, you'll be feeling better by morning." Then he asked, "You really ate that animal rare?"

Danish turned back from the window. "I told him to put it back on …"

Doc Thorndyke dug into his bag and produced a powder-filled glass tube. "This'll stop you up for three days, guaranteed. Dissolve it in water morning and night. Make sure you pack a lot of water—you need to rehydrate, starting now. I understand you're headed to Fort Worth. That'll be a three-day ride, at least. Skip a dose the night before you expect to arrive, so you can empty before your journey resumes."

"He'll follow your orders, Doc," Danish promised. "What about food? The missus downstairs offered rice."

"That's fine. Biscuits for dinner. By tomorrow morning, hash. After that, trail food should be tolerable. But take it easy—no coon!"

"Heavens no," Sam agreed.

"How much do we owe you?" asked Danish.

"A dollar for the remedy is all. If I need to come again, I'll charge for the visit."

"We's much obliged—ain't we, Sam?"

"Much."

Danish paid the man and saw him downstairs. After a few minutes he returned with the proprietress and her promised bowl of steaming rice. Roy brought a pitcher of water. He helped Sam prop himself up in bed. Then, seeing the woman out, he thanked her for her trouble.

"I'll have those biscuits steaming hot," she said.

Danish closed the door and poured Sam a tall glass of water, setting it on the night table. He returned to the armchair and watched Sam chew. Spirits raised, the youth was already looking better. Finally, Roy got up and spilled some water into the hand bowl on the dresser, then cupped a handful and slapped his face with it. Patting his mustache dry with the cloth, he took another glance out the window, expecting to see the absence of Reddy and Bo's rig.

Yet there it still was on the opposite landing. The lead animals were now attached, but there was no sign of the men.

Danish was beginning to worry when a horse and rider suddenly appeared on the far bank before plunging into the river. Grasping the window sill, he sharpened his focus. Was that Bo? His size was right. Wasn't that Bo's flimsy hat too?

And those flashes on his chest—made by his suspender buckles? "Downright strange," he observed aloud.

"What is, Roy?"

Danish discerned the red of the braces, and turned back to Sam. "Bo's a-crossing back!" he concluded before looking again.

The rider—now up to his knees in the river—was angling his crossing toward Ben Ficklin, instead of heading straight for the landing.

"He's making a beeline for town ..."

Sam paused between chews. "Maybe he forgot something in his room."

Danish nodded. "I best check."

He stepped out to try the door across the hall, and found it unlocked. The door creaked open, revealing a bed already made and a full pitcher beside a wash-pot on the dresser. He stooped to search under the bed, then got up to open the dresser drawers. Nothing. Crossing back to his room, he grabbed his hat and told Sam he'd meet Bo on the road. Then he left and thumped down the stairs, where he found the bespectacled hotel owner absorbed in the town one-sheet.

"Pardon my asking," said Danish, "but was anything found in my partners' room?"

The proprietor rose, yanking off his reading glasses. "Them that checked out? We would've informed you. Something wrong, mister?"

"It's just that one of 'em is crossing back."

"Crossing the river?"

Danish fitted his hat on his head. "I'm gonna see what it's about ..."

Chapter Thirteen

With pinched lips and closed eyes, she drew a long breath through her nose. "The river is near …"

Dismounted, they resumed pushing through a patch of tangled, thorny brush, Chivatá again in the lead. Even in such a place, Renald found himself admiring her figure as she twisted and turned through the brambles; but a rude barb to his side—like nature's elbow—abruptly delivered a correction. They soon came to a small clearing, beyond which the waters of the South Concho glittered through a wall of branches and bushes. From the river came a cool breeze, a balm after the scrapes and scratches their journey had inflicted.

Renald's horse shied back with a whinny, causing him to grip the reins closer to the animal's jaw. Was there something threatening in the wind? Fear spread to Chivatá's mare, her head jerking in protest. Both horses flattened their ears.

"Careful," Renald whispered.

Matter-of-factly, Chivatá responded. "Why? He's dead."

In stunned ignorance, he puckered his lips to ask, "Who?"

At the same moment, he spotted the corpse at her feet.

Pants down around his ankles, a white man lay on his back, his member exposed in a tuft of red hair. An arrow's rigid shaft protruded from his blood-soaked shirt. The young man's face was spattered with glistening chaw.

"That's some way to go—pissing into a bush," said Renald. "Damned if I'll ever do it again."

Remaining still, he scanned the area. No sign of company here. Further on toward the river, he registered a tarp-covered, mule-drawn buckboard.

"Buffalo skins," she said, her voice rough with tension.

"I smell them too," he replied.

The team of animals had dragged the rig to a natural grazing spot of riverside grass. A riderless saddle horse hung his head there, chomping as well.

Peering down at the victim, Chivatá said, "Endah's arrows are longer. This one bears the marks of the Northern People."

"The medicine man's sons," Renald deduced. "But they didn't scalp him. Why?"

Crouching to the right of the body, she seemed to pick up their trail. "There wasn't time …" She swept her finger northward.

"Maybe not," he said. "But how come they didn't retrieve the arrow? Can't be packing too many."

Chivatá stood up, exasperated. "You know nothing about the Apache, do you?"

Palms up, he confessed, "Next to nothing."

"An Apache arrow tastes blood once," she explained impatiently, "and only once."

"In my culture, we have rules against double dipping too." With that, he started for the rig.

She raised her hand, cautioning, "Step carefully … Everything is written on the ground."

He halted as if before quicksand, pivoting at the waist. "Well, where *don't* I step?"

Chivatá made an expert visual sweep of the area, ending somewhere to Renald's right, where the foliage was denser. Then, moving beyond the corpse, she cat-stepped past Renald to the buckboard. Combing the ground with her gaze, she crisscrossed the general area, here and there squatting to examine something—a line of tracks, a broken twig, a blade of stray prairie grass. She was establishing not just where the others went, Renald noted, but the sequence of their movements, the history of the event. Finally, she wheeled about and passed Renald—frozen in his tracks—and headed for the wagon.

"Can I move now?" he asked irritably. When she didn't answer he shrugged, staying put.

Next, inspecting a grassy area past the rig and near the riverbank, she seemed to find something. Righting herself and turning southwest, she cast her view toward the opposite side—onto Ben Ficklin.

* * *

Danish threw open the hotel doors, strode off the boardwalk, and marched down Main Street toward the river. On his left he passed the bank, the mercantile, and the newspaper office. On his right, the signs read *Wayward Saloon, Saddlery,* and *Telegraph Office;* and there too, was the clothier where Bo had purchased those telltale suspenders. Many people were out and about already; lots of hat-tipping in the amber glow of dawn. But when he rounded the corner onto the Fort Concho road, he was met by empty air.

Hands on hips, he squinted northward. Where in God's name had Bo gone?

A short distance up the road was the boat landing with its unmistakable town sign, the flatboat tethered to shore. Over his left shoulder, the grazing fields lay reduced and trampled after the dawn beef pullout. He searched far across the open plain without finding any trace of movement. That presented two possibilities. Either Bo had cut diagonally into town—toward the livery?—or he'd somehow aborted his mission and returned to the rig while Danish was scrambling to intercept him.

Danish fretted. If Bo had left nothing behind, maybe he'd dropped something along the way and gone back for it—maybe his bedroll had washed downstream, something like that. "I'm shooting in the dark," the skinner conceded to himself, "and that ain't no way to hunt game." He clicked his tongue in frustration. Should he go back to the hotel or over to the livery? Or should he hire out that barge to take him to the other side? From where he stood, he could see the two boat operators outside their shed, turning their hatted heads east to west and back again—equally confounded, it seemed to him.

Across the river, the butt of the rig jutted from a gap in the trees. Danish focused so hard on it that he failed to notice a figure crouching to its left, obscured by high grass. No movement over there, he concluded. No unusual sounds. He cupped his hands and called out, "Bo! … Reddy!"

In the silence that followed, he tore his hat off and rubbed his fingers through his hair. Still nothing. A growing sense of urgency caused him to call out once more. Then, perplexed by the lack of response, he switched his focus back to the riverside landing ahead, where one of the men was pointing his way.

Making eye contact, Danish started for them. It lasted for just a second or two, before—

* * *

On hearing a stranger's calls from the other side, Chivatá instinctively sought deeper concealment in the waist-high grass bordering the river, then made her way over to Renald.

"There are four, not three, sets of tracks," she explained. "Three made by Indian ponies and one made by moccasin boots. All the ponies went that way ..." She pointed northward again. "But there are fresh moccasin tracks from where you just stepped. They lead straight to the water."

"So?"

She continued like a trooper delivering a report. "Endah arrived on his pony first. When he did, no one was here. But I think he saw these men crossing."

"*Men?*" Renald gestured toward the lone, grazing stray horse.

Without acknowledging his observation, she continued, "Endah avoided them and headed north. Soon after, the white men came to this side. That man fell first." She gestured toward Reddy's body. "The other man," she said, "lies in the grass behind me."

Cursing, Renald stepped past her to look for the second victim.

"Maybe he screamed," she added, rotating as he went by. "Because something triggered Endah to circle wide back without his pony, probably to learn if he was being pursued."

Renald found the second body, and lingered over it. Arrow-shot through the neck and lying face up, it was naked except for a pair of shorts. The man's pop eyes and his gaping mouth, spilling blood, revealed the horror of his death.

Beside his body, Renald noticed, lay a wide bow and a quiver stuffed with very long arrows. Never before had he seen an Indian arrow like that.

"Endah made his choice," Chivatá said.

Confused, Renald responded "Choice? What choice?"

"The arrow that killed this man is also Northern," she said. "But the ones you see here are too long for Apache arrows, and yet they bear our markings and feathers." She paused as if for effect. "They are Endah's."

For a moment Renald was speechless: an abandoned bow and quiver beside a white man's corpse stripped of its clothing. What a sight. Finally, he said, "Tall Grass did say Endah carried a great bow or something like that. Here it is …"

"I must tell him that Endah is Karl again."

Renald eyeballed Ben Ficklin as his mind worked. Before long, he became aware of two men on the opposite landing. Barge operators scrutinizing them from a boathouse labelled *Ben Ficklin.* Had the bargemen heard a scream? Surely they'd witnessed the boy crossing to their side. Now one of them gestured southward, and Renald noticed a third figure marching up the road from town.

"You're wrong," he said, turning back to Chivatá. "He didn't steal clothes off a dead man to become white again. No … He's disguised himself as a white man to blend in, to disappear. He's a smart one."

She grinned coolly. "So are you, *Capitán.*"

"Retired," he replied.

* * *

Splash. Across the river from Danish, a pair of riders plunged their mounts side by side into the South Concho, exhorting their animals forward with lashes and cries, and sending ripples downstream. They were midway across when Danish realized that one of them was a woman—a squaw riding saddle. "I'll be damned," he muttered. They would reach the boat landing before he could.

Dragging himself forward, he watched as the two crossed in front of the moored flatboat and rose onto the riverbank, their animals shedding sheets of water. The male rider exchanged words with the boat operators, who in turn gestured in Danish's direction. The riders immediately reined toward him, their hoofbeats reaching a gallop pitch. Brave though he was, Danish felt naked without a gun.

He began making slow-down signals with his hands.

As if in response, the woman yanked rein, causing her fellow rider to pull back as well. Instead of trotting toward Danish, she reversed a step or two, leaning from the saddle horn and indicating something on the ground. From his mount, the white man examined whatever had seized her attention. She drew a line with her hand from the riverbank toward town.

Danish wouldn't have missed the wet tracks either.

"Hey there!" he cried, coming forward. "You following that fella just crossed the river?"

The male rider, square-jawed and seasoned, sat his mount with an air of courtliness. Despite his civilian dress, to Danish he had Army written all over him.

"Well, that's my partner, Bo! Bobby Granger," Danish explained.

In a faint southern drawl, the rider asked, "How can you be sure?"

Danish stood stock-still with alarm. "Well, he rode over from that rig, ain't he?" When the stranger nodded, he continued,

"And he was wearing shiny suspenders like Bo done. His voice cracked. "Anything wrong?"

After a quick glance at the woman, the rider replied, "I'd say so. But count yourself lucky. That man isn't your friend Bo."

"*Lucky that man isn't your friend Bo*" is how Danish heard it. He felt himself flush. "But I just told you …" He stopped to shuffle his thoughts. Then, hooking imaginary suspenders with his thumbs, he continued, "See, I recognized him by his duds."

The riders traded looks a second time, registering something between them. Now Danish noticed the Indian's allure—albeit fleetingly, because the man with her quickly turned back to him.

"That wasn't your friend you saw crossing the river," he said.

Danish felt himself breathless. "It wudn't?"

"If you'd been over there with him, you'd be dead too."

"*Dead?*"

"No time to explain," the rider responded. "Just don't cross without a posse—there's Apache in those woods, and they're probably doubling back right about now."

* * *

After the two galloped off toward Ben Ficklin, Danish looked around confoundedly. Somehow, through his mental haze, a simple deduction emerged: if Bo and Reddy were in fact deceased, the man he'd spotted wearing Bo's braces could be their killer. But were his friends really dead? And how did that rider and his woman scout fit into it? Too many questions for now. First things first. He must cross to the other side.

The two boat operators were angling toward him on the road. Bounding forward, he yelled, "You got a gun? Take me across!"

Part III

The Men

Chapter Fourteen

As a boy he'd played Cowboys and Indians with Freddie—in the room they shared with their parents, on the porch, in the fields. Conflicts never arose over who got which part. Freddie, being enamored of their *Vati*'s stories of the Second Schleswig War, was always the patriotic horse soldier, whereas Karl— his shirt thrown aside and his face painted reluctantly by his *Mutti*—was ever the bloodthirsty warrior.

When they were taken some three summers ago, Freddie cowered and trembled as would any nine-year-old during their days of hard-riding transit to the Northern People's camp. His elder brother Karl, on the other hand, had put up such a ceaseless and spirited resistance that his captors came to admire him. In fact, his toughness increased his value.

Principal among the young Apaches entrusted with Karl's taming was the spirit man's eldest son, later called Burnt Face.

Eventually, Endah would realize that Freddie's rescue by the cavalry had been the best thing for both boys. For his meek brother, recapture was truly lifesaving. But for himself, the sudden loss of Freddie—though it had left him alone among his abductors—became another kind of liberation. To survive among the Indians, a boy must molt his white skin as he grows, and in time Endah grew completely out of Karl. He came to revel in the hunt, the skinning, the drinking of buffalo blood and marrow, the camaraderie, the sex.

His intention upon fleeing the Lipan village was just as Renald had suspected—to reach Comanche country north of Fort Concho. There Endah planned to seek sanctuary with the very band to which he'd traded a black girl not long ago. Unless they had moved camp, he could find them. The last of the Llano Comanche were in desperate need of able young men. As he'd reported to Chief Tall Grass, this small band planned to combine with a larger one expected from the reservation. He might be able to join up as well.

The bodies by the river changed that plan. He had guessed the shaman's sons would pursue him, and to him those corpses were the proof. Their tracks revealed that they went northward after him into the thicket. Soon they would discover his wandering pony, identify his trail, and double back to find the white man stripped. Then what? Endah couldn't imagine Burnt Face merely shrugging his shoulders. Instead, he would exercise the survival instincts possessed by every Apache raider, only this time projected onto one with white skin. That meant he would guess Endah's new destination and try to overtake him on the wide-open country between here and there.

To avert the trappers' fate by riding for town disguised as one—that is, as a paleface—Endah was exercising his natural advantage while consciously playing white for the first time. He'd even stuffed his long hair into his newly acquired hat. It hid his headband too. Scared though he was, with the backside of Ben Ficklin looming larger on his left, he felt some amusement, pride even, in riding saddle with a gun on his hip. Amusement and pride—yes; power and ability, no. Truth be told, he wasn't competent with the weapon. Only older braves like Burnt Face had the privilege of being experienced shots, but even they preferred traditional arms for their stealth.

Indeed, only a single, fleeting human cry had alerted Endah to the fateful encounter on the river bank.

These were his musings as he crossed the South Concho and started onto the trampled fields beside the town. Yes, he had put a river between himself and his pursuers—a boundary they would not cross by day—but what was he to do with himself in town? Perhaps he should steer clear of it, and instead ride southward for the faraway Ghost Mountains. Whatever his decision, Burnt Face, using the same logic, would surmise it— of that, he was sure. In Endah's mind there was no escaping the elder son of the spirit man, except by surrounding himself with white people.

His brow began to sweat under his hidden headband.

Now hoofbeats. Behind him.

He jerked his mount around. Between here and the river a dust boil was rising, a pair of galloping horses stirring it up. The healer's sons? Impossible. Even Burnt Face wouldn't be so bold. Fretting, he ground his teeth. Somebody else had found the bodies, then. Those boatmen? But there hadn't been time for that, he told himself. Whatever this was about, he must disappear. He swung his horse around again and rode along the backsides of the single and two-story structures along Main Street. Finally, he led her between buildings to the bustling town center—noisy with creaking four-wheelers, people's chatter, the knocks of incessant hammering, and presently a ringing church bell.

Instinct dictated that he lead his mount toward the river, rather than away from it as if in flight. Crossing to the other side of the street, he blended in with the easterly traffic while avoiding any eye contact, lest somebody recognize the Indian in him. Though his heart was pounding like a drum, and his hands fidgeted with the reins in his lap, by sitting straight in his saddle he did his best to appear natural. His concealed headband kept the sweat from coating his face.

Confident he wouldn't be spotted from behind, and that his tracks were lost in the mangled dirt, he allowed himself a liberal scan of Main Street. He was struck by its familiarity. This could have been his hometown of Mason, and he might've been seeing it from the back of a wagon on a supply trip with his parents. At once he remembered the shopping stops, the money changing hands, the street dust, and a certain Mr. Wilcox at the General Store who always rewarded him and his brother with a peppermint stick each. Being the younger, Freddie always got his first. "You boys have yourselves a sweet one!" Mr. Wilcox would always say, thumbing his suspenders as the boys sucked their candies. The memory stirred the juices in Endah's mouth.

Filled with nostalgia, he thumbed one of his own newly acquired suspenders. A town visit had always been an event for his brother and himself, a wonderous break from their endless chores. But as he trotted down the street this day, his heart began to race. For how should he conduct himself here, and for how long could he maintain the act? What if somebody talked to him!

Yet, although this situation was perplexing, experiencing a mixed sense of peril and wonderment wasn't unusual: he often felt heightened emotions on the hunt. Once, disguised in a calf's hide while stalking a stray buffalo, he had unexpectedly found himself absorbed into the drifting herd. The other braves, conscious of his predicament, backed off, and he was left alone among the beasts, baking for what seemed hours in the heavy hide. Afraid to lift his head and nauseated by the stench, he could do nothing but wait for the animals to move on, around him thudding hooves, snorts and blows, grunts and gurgles, and the ceaseless murmur of feeding. A peaceful calm that promised death if he was detected.

Clang, clang—clang, clang. The bell continued to ring. He was losing his cover as the prayer-summons began draining the street of townsfolk.

And yet it never occurred to him that his best chance of survival was simply to march into the nearest store and identify himself as Karl Hermann, that long-lost boy from Loyal Valley. Glancing ahead, he was rewarded with a courteous nod from a passing stranger. Instinctively averting his eyes, Endah noticed a mother and daughter on the opposite side, strolling down the boardwalk in fancy wool and lace—rigid in their corsets, clean and collected. By the time such women were brought to the Indian camp, they were anything but.

Deciding to abandon his horse, he angled himself toward a building whose sign read *Hotel.* Quite unaware that his approach was being followed from a second-floor window, he entered the shade cast by the overhang.

"Bo!" came a cry from above. "Bo, lookie here!"

To Endah, the entreaty was just another addition to the unnerving cacophony. Glancing sideways, he alighted from the saddle, then hitched the horse.

Since he had no idea who was trying to overtake him, he didn't know what to look for—except two riders in a hurry.

Resting a hand on the horse's haunch, he angled his view back up Main Street, where a pair of riders had entered the fray, drawing the attention of bystanders. A crowd gathered around them like flies. The reason for this became obvious when Endah saw that one of them was a fellow Apache. Even at this distance he could discern the headband and the parted black hair.

He shied back in a rush of fear. Could it be Burnt Face? He studied the figure, concluding it was not. And who was the paleface? A white man with an Apache guide? Endah sucked his lower lip. *A captive hunter and his scout,* he concluded. *They must've found the bodies.*

Meantime, the open church doors continued to draw people in from the street, threatening to expose him. *No,* he thought desperately, *they won't recognize me in these dead man's clothes. How could they? But they will look for a wet horse.* He became aware of the still-moist fur under his left hand, and the horse's quivering muscles as it shifted its weight.

Water. Water spots on the mare's neck and rump. He put it all together: they were tracking him by the runoff. He shot a look down at the hooves. Yes, the ground below was splotched with water. He'd squeezed off some when he dismounted.

Up Main Street, the riders had now broken free of the crowd. Through the traffic, he glimpsed the Apache warrior on a grey-spotted pony, pointing at the ground and leading the other rider into the road. Just where had he seen that pony before? Endah didn't wait to find out. His shifting gaze found a storefront labelled *General Store.* Though the name was incomprehensible to him, there was a familiarity about those two words, something inviting, even.

Chin down, he moved toward it.

* * *

Just as the hustle and bustle of Main Street had presented Endah with a familiar and yet dismaying experience, the store interior did as well—so many objects of different shapes and sizes, stacked, rowed, jarred, barreled. Casting a shy glance at the counter off to his left, he registered behind it a big-bellied, bespectacled man in a smudged apron, busy measuring spices for a bonnet-topped woman. No one else seemed to be around. True to his memories—indeed, to his lasting fondness for such places—there on the counter, under the shopkeeper's very nose, were jars of candies that instantly recalled his childhood. One of the glass jars, catching the light, was stuffed with those red- and white-striped sticks he so loved. Endah could almost taste the tart mint on his tongue, followed by a concentrated sweetness unlike any he'd experienced since—utterly different from berries, squash, honey or sap. A rush of nostalgia overcame him as he remembered his brother in the back of their parents' bumpy buckboard. Once more he was picturing the kind Mr. Wilcox. Finally, he saw the evening hearth fire of home.

Home?

In haste, he ducked into one of the rows of stock before him—calf-skin gloves and gardening tools and a number of things whose uses escaped him and whose strangeness increased his unease.

What to do here? This was no desert outcropping to hide behind.

After a brief verbal exchange between the shopkeeper and his customer, the bell over the door rang open and shut. Now, quite alone in the store with the proprietor, a feeling of panic seized him. He hastened for the exit.

Before he could reach it, the white man was calling out something.

Endah thought he understood. Yet how should he respond? He could shrug the man off and instead take his chances in the street. Which was the greater danger? His hesitation produced a reminder of those mint sticks.

Digging in his pocket, he played with a large coin he found there. Its value was a mystery, but its utility wasn't. It could buy him some time too. He recalled exchanging coin for candy in Mason, and receiving change in return.

The cherubic man behind the counter wore a quizzical, indulgent smile as Endah came close.

Endah dipped his chin at the jar.

"Why, sure thing!" the man reacted, glancing aslant. "Just one stick, then?" He lifted a finger in the air.

"Yah," Endah heard himself say.

"New to the country, I take it. Welcome to Ben Ficklin!" Waiting for his meaning to register, the man sustained a grin.

Willkommen, thought Endah. *"Danke,"* he mumbled at last, forcing up the corners of his mouth.

The man clawed into the jar with a sheet of wax paper. "Got any brothers or sisters?"

Mein Bruder, thought Endah. *"Ja, einen Bruder."*

"All right, then," the man responded. He began wrapping a pair of sticks. "The extra's on me! For your brother. Anything else?"

Tentatively, Endah offered the coin. The man took it between the fingers of one hand while extending the packet in the other.

As the man moved toward the cash register, revealed on the wall display behind him were a bow and a buckskin quiver stuffed with arrows, some of them three-feathered Lipan Apache.

"I want," was all Endah could say in English, nodding. He shoved the mints into a pocket.

Sliding the change across the counter, the proprietor pivoted toward the items. "You mean the bow and arrows?" He mimicked pulling the bowstring, his eyes pinning Endah over his shoulder.

Endah nodded.

"Well, son—I can let you have the whole set for, say, three dollars?"

Endah cocked his head, at a loss. Then, thinking fast, he unbuckled the gunsling on his hip and plunked it down on the counter between them.

A tentative moment followed. Their eyes met. The man, his chest expanding with an opportunistic breath, seized the gun butt and ripped the pistol from its holster. He released and spun the full chamber. Though not much of a gun, it was an irresistible trade.

"You got yourself a deal, young man!"

After setting the weapon down on its side, he unhooked the items one by one and pushed them across the counter.

Without pause, Endah spilled out the arrows and rapidly separated out the good ones, testing the hardness of the wood, the straightness of the shafts, and the tightness of the arrowhead sinew bindings. He even straightened one shaft between his teeth.

The proprietor observed, astonished. "You some sort of hobbyist?"

Endah reloaded the quiver, strapped it on, and shouldered the bow.

He was turning toward the exit when the storekeeper heaved a wooden box onto the counter from below—a well-intentioned but potentially grave mistake.

"Have your pick o' them! No charge …"

Endah found himself looking down at a collection of long-haired scalps.

"This one here's Comanche," said the man, referring to one with a scalp lock. He reached in and exposed its pale backside. "Most of them's Apache. All scrubbed clean!"

Endah was about to reach for his new weapon when the door opened with a ring.

Startled, he suppressed the impulse. A glint in the storekeeper's eye caused Endah to turn in his stolen boots toward the new commotion.

Entering with swishing grace while the storekeeper hastily stowed the box were the mother and daughter pair from outside. They seemed to glide forward in their ankle-length dresses.

"Well, if it isn't the Harvey ladies!" the man exclaimed. "Aren't you two a sight!"

While the rouged woman, in front, responded with red, upturned lips, the unpainted girl answered Endah's stare with a cool look. He was, after all, armed like an Indian. To his eyes, by contrast, she was a spectacular vision—so fine and clean and doll-like. Brushing past him with a flowery, enveloping fragrance, she offered a barely perceptible expression of—was it amusement or attraction?

In her presence he felt even more awkward than he had before on the street. He felt inadequate.

As if by intention, her strange yet tantalizing scent twisted into a prickly weapon inside his nose, and he doubled over, sneezing with explosive intensity. This only increased his anxiety, and he failed to find words of apology that she could understand. Righting himself, he withdrew a step like a jumpy street cat, knocking over something—a tinny thud behind him, a roll. He blushed with embarrassment. With that, a smile played on the girl's lips.

"Oops," she said, glancing over her frilled shoulder, cheeks high.

Only moments ago, he'd been a twitch away from killing the storekeeper. Now he shot the man a petrified look.

"No harm done, young buck! You have yourself a day!"

Stepping toward the door, Endah felt the girl's delicate presence receding, and a surprising melancholy arose in him that supplanted the thrill of their brief encounter. He felt himself conflicted between the urge to hang back for her and the imperative to make his escape, and yet both urges were consistent with his tribal education to take and run.

Back of him, the storekeeper was striking up a conversation with Mrs. Harvey. Endah moved ahead, his every step feeling fateful.

The view through the glass stopped him. A familiar form and gait, a presence. Was it possible? Across the way, below the sign reading *Hotel,* the Apache warrior he'd seen from afar just minutes before had dismounted and was taking her place beside a tall, lean man in a pushed-back hat tied below his chin. Yes, taking *her* place. Now shockingly apparent, she was none other than the Lipan woman warrior Chivatá—a favorite of Chief Tall Grass. As for her companion, more than anything else it was the chin-tie that recalled him to Endah. This was the selfsame paleface who'd raided the Northern People camp with the army, the very man who had thrown Burnt Face into the fire and rescued Freddie. Without a doubt, this was the man for whom Endah had prayed all those months thereafter. Here he was at last. Yet the Indian captive that "Chin-tie" was seeking had vanished. Vanished, like grains of sand into the winds of time.

The two of them, half encircled by onlookers—some saddled, others on foot—were hearing out a yellow-haired youth on the hotel landing. As the crowd shifted, Endah saw that the boy wore boots over what appeared to be full-body underwear, red in color.

The youth—not much older than himself—was pointing toward an open window on the hotel's second floor; then he jabbed northeast in the direction of the barge landings. Suddenly, Straw Hair thrust his finger toward Endah, cowering here behind the pane of glass.

Chivatá and Chin-tie both drew their sidearms.

In the shop, Endah jerked backward.

"Anything wrong, boy?" asked the storekeeper.

Unheeding, Endah—his jaw slackening—watched as Chivatá and Chin-tie advanced from across the street, weapons drawn. Behind them, Straw Hair protested, "Don't do it! What if it's Bo?"

As the boy stepped forward, some townsfolk followed him while others held back. Still others looked for cover.

Breaking into a sweat, Endah withdrew into the store's interior with the realization that the very clothes allowing him to blend in now identified him. He began scanning the shelves for something to change into.

"What is it, son?" The proprietor's voice had thickened.

He needed a back door as well. But then it struck him that he hadn't a chance without a horse—and only out front were there horses, plenty of them. Fretting, he realized that minutes ago he could've just kept riding, undetected, toward the river.

With feverish eyes, he glanced again toward the hotel.

Luckily for him, Chivatá and her companion were impeded in their attempt to cross the street by a mass of apprehensive locals coalescing in a tightening circle around them, voices and fists raised. In an attempt to break through them, the tall man waved a piece of paper.

Endah seized his chance.

Like a wild creature bolting from a cage, he banged out the door and leapt over the hitch rail and into the street. Gasps sprang from the crowd. Hitting the ground running, he ripped an arrow from the quiver strapped to his back.

In seconds—long to him, short to the others—he found a shot straight into the neck of Chivatá's pony.

The animal reared with a monstrous cry and a burst of blood that, as she swung wildly to one side, showered the scattering, screaming, stumbling mass of people. The beast's extreme pivot caused her hind hooves to slip, sending her bulk crashing backwards into other mounts tethered to the hotel hitch. The thudding contact was followed by distressed neighs and snorts, and the force of the spooked animals snapped the rail like a twig. A couple of horses, including the dead Bo's mare, stormed the boardwalk.

Clouds of dust enveloped the hammering throng. Meantime, Endah slung his new bow over his shoulder and gave a running start at one fleeing horse. He managed to gain purchase of the saddle horn, heaved himself into the saddle, and grabbed the reins.

Though a head start was critical to his escape, he couldn't help but perform some mischief in parting—he was sixteen, after all. By this time, the storekeeper and the Harvey women had hastened outside to witness the incident. Endah, partly to impress the stunned girl and partly to repel her because he could, reined the horse around while removing his hat to expose his Apache headband to all. Hair dropping like a curtain over his shoulders, he made the Apache war cry. Then, discarding the white man's hat in disgust, he kicked his new mount into a gallop toward the river. All in the street were left groping and coughing in the dust. At last, out of this melée staggered Chivatá and Scott Renald, caked with dirt and spattered with horse blood.

Chivatá immediately raced to her writhing pony, yet another victim of Renald's intervention into Apache affairs. No tears followed. Without visible emotion, she took the prescribed action and a shot from her revolver put the animal down. The dead thing was a last physical reminder that Nalen was gone too.

* * *

When the dapple grey went down, Renald's first thought was *it could've been us*. At any moment while they stood exposed in the street, Karl might've lunged out that storefront and tried to sink some arrows into them. He didn't. That he struck the pony instead gave Renald a degree of hope. Maybe the boy had mixed feelings. Maybe he could be taken without a fight.

While Renald helped the youngster in long johns to his feet, Chivatá volunteered to round up their remaining horse—a sign of willing cooperation that did not escape him.

The young man was wide-eyed. "It's just like you said! That wasn't Bo."

Renald asked him for his name, and then braced him by the shoulders. "Sam, I'm afraid your partners across the river are dead. Are you able to listen?"

Choking up, words failing him, Sam could only nod, glassy-eyed.

Chivatá appeared at Renald's side with their remaining horse, the crowd gathering around them.

"Get yourself—or get somebody here—to the telegraph office," Renald told Sam. "Send the following message to Fort Sill *and* Fort Richardson! *Scott Renald says breakout imminent at Fort Sill.*"

He made Sam repeat the message. The youth, stammering with terror, stumbled over the word "imminent," and Renald made him say it again.

"Now say my name!"

"Your name is *Scott Renald.*"

"You got it. Good luck!"

Renald was first to mount, with Chivatá swinging up behind and embracing his midsection. The horse gave a halting start under the added weight, then bounded powerfully toward the river, the town a fast-moving blur at their sides. Way ahead, Karl hit the water in a burst of spray. A minute later, Renald drew rein at the riverbank, his lean back countered by the push of Chivatá's body. By this time Karl had nearly reached the other side through agitated waters a shoulder's depth to his horse.

Renald eased out of Chivatá's hold, standing in his stirrups and cupping his hands. "Karl, stop!" he cried. "Let's talk!"

When the boy didn't respond, Chivatá called after him in the Apache language—but the horse and rider heedlessly drove up the opposing riverbank.

Renald fired a warning shot. The report echoed. But Karl kept pushing ahead. Renald jogged the reins, and they plunged into the river. A distracted moment followed as Renald felt his boots fill with water. "Get a shot off over my back," he told Chivatá. "Aim for his horse!"

He bent forward over his mount's thrusting neck while Chivatá took aim across his back. But in this position the gun barrel became aligned with the animal's head, and the report that followed exploded like cannon fire in its ear. The next instant, Renald and Chivatá found themselves deservedly in the river.

Renald saw a browned, liquid sky behind a dispersing mass of bubbles. Luckily, he'd been able to clear both stirrups. He rose on his feet, broke the surface, and grabbed his hat before it got away. Chivatá was next up, gasping for air, water coursing down her face. Aware that most Indians did not swim, Renald pushed toward her. But she surprised him by grabbing hold of his horse's tail and gliding past him as the beast made for shore. *Nice trick*, he thought, clumsily wading after her. Soon they both collapsed onto the grassy bank.

She drew her gun and drained it of water.

Renald, flattening his back on the ground, gave it a stretch— squinting into the cloudless blanket of blue above. Then, as if mocking their soaked gunpowder, an eruption of gunfire sounded upriver. Renald turned to Chivatá beside him. "Was that boy wearing a gun? I sure didn't see one …"

Chapter Fifteen

At Fort Richardson, Lieutenant Colonel John Davidson was starting his last week commanding the 10th Cavalry. It was seven a.m., and Black Jack was just in receipt of an alert from Fort Sill in Indian Territory to the north. An as yet unknown number of warriors and their families, led by the Kotsoteka leader Teneverka, had left the reserve under cover of darkness. No less than fifty horses were missing from the fort's corral, rendering Colonel MacKenzie unable to lead a mounted pursuit.

Normally Davidson would have called his remaining captain, Norton, to his office. Norton, however, had gone with A Company to relieve Fort Concho, whose troops were out patrolling the Rio Grande to stem cross-border Indian incursions. Sergeant Chance and C Troop had stayed here to decommission the post. On Thursday this week Davidson himself would set out for Fort Custer, Montana, putting his many proud years with the 10th Cavalry behind him.

Since Davidson's capture in 1874 of what was destined to be the last great Comanche and Kiowa camp, he and his fellow regimental commanders had achieved relative security for the settler, the cowboy, and the hunter alike in what they called "dry country." But as the army was lately diverting its resources to more volatile areas—further south and west into Apacheria and north into Cheyenne and Sioux country—enterprising hostile bands had started to exploit the gaps in patrol coverage of the Llano Estacado. Settlers and skinners had been slaughtered, livestock and other possessions looted. Of special concern to the army was that bands of Mescalero and Chiricahua Apache, among others, had lately been joining with Comanche holdouts in Texas, while Geronimo and Caballero were engaging in hostilities across the border in New Mexico Territory. Hence the urgency of the peace talks at Washington, initiated by an assortment of newly confident headmen, and now the exigency of a decisive military response to the Sill breakout.

Upon receiving the cable in his half-emptied office, Davidson sent word to Sergeant Chance to meet him in the communications station. There, they huddled over the telegraph and its operator, who sent messages forth and back between them and Captain Norton at Fort Concho. Davidson, his hands flattened on opposite sides of the wired conductor tub, could see in its still water the reflection of his own chin-whiskered face on this side, and the operator's tense brow on the other.

"Inform the captain," he ordered, "that Colonel Mackenzie has given Talking Moon and a small Comanche delegation a pass to locate and parley with the breakouts. Talking Moon is en route on remaining army mounts to Ox Creek supply point posthaste." Eyeing Chance, he said, "You will meet them there."

Chance clicked his heels, snapping straight the yellow piping of his uniform. "Yessir. But what about the fort, sir?"

"This fort?" The post had been quickly overtaken by settlement and was virtually useless these days, except as a launching point. For Davidson, it was easy to dismiss. "We'll leave a few men here. When the situation is under control, you'll return to tear it down. I'll draft the order."

Thus, Captain Norton and A Troop would ride north to establish a supply base at Ox Creek, with Chance and C Troop riding southwest to effect a juncture with him there. Chance might even reach the rendezvous point before Talking Moon could.

"Now listen closely," said Davidson. "We know that Apache and Comanche elements are joining forces on the Llano— Chiricahua and Mescalero are fleeing the San Carlos reservation in Arizona, and responding to pressure from Fort Stanton in New Mexico. They're all in fighting spirit and fifty or more mounted Comanche mixing in won't help. A tussle with them could compromise the present Apache negotiations at Washington."

"Respectfully, it's rare there ain't a tussle when we attempt a removal."

Davidson was firm. "Avoid one at all costs. Tell Captain Norton I so advised. The press will turn the slightest action into a battle, and a battle into a war. These days, the Indian lobby reads newspapers too. The press'll spoil everything to sell papers, and could cause the frontier to roll back on us. Do your best to restrain Norton. He's in a bad way since Alice passed."

"I'll try," said Chance with a sigh.

Davidson raised his finger. "The captain should remember his error of '72 that practically ended in a court martial."

"Ain't my place, sir …"

"Well, don't you rely on chasing Indians. Tracks are less reliable than *this*." He tapped his temple. "This time of year, buffalo are known to gather at Cedar Lake and Farther Lake.

That means hostiles too. How soon can you call 'Boots and Saddles?' "

"It'll take a day to rustle up the provisions."

"We don't have a day, Tops." Davidson gestured toward the door.

"Could be a long scout," said Chance. Stepping outside, he squinted aloft. "And a scorched one at that."

"Take as many barrels as you need."

"Wheels will slow us down, sir."

Clapping his first sergeant's shoulders, Davidson said, "Don't be too polite with me, Tops. I'm anxious enough without all those unnecessary 'sirs.' I'll leave the logistics to you."

Chance adjusted his footing. "But what if …" His voice trailed off.

"Sergeant?"

"Well … I can't help wondering if Talking Moon ain't behind it all."

Davidson dismissed the idea with a huff. "Behind the breakout? Ridiculous."

Chance took the dismissal in stride. "Apache throwing in with the Comanche out there might not be a coincidence. Talking Moon's a cunning Indian if there ever was one."

"Talking Moon's a big man on the reservation—the biggest," Davidson replied. "He profits from peace. Believe me."

"I do," said Chance. "I just don't trust *him*."

The telegraph operator came crashing out of his office. He thudded down the steps, leather heels creaking the planks. A sudden gust mussed his hair. Blinking behind thick, round lenses, he told them, "From Scott Renald in Ben Ficklin. He's warning us of the Sill breakout, sir."

Davidson snatched the scribbled note, glanced at it. "How'd *he* hear about it? We only just found out ourselves."

Chance gave it some thought. "Far out as Ben Ficklin means he rode straight through Lipan country."

Davidson smoothed his whiskers. "If the Lipan were informed in advance, then how? Why?" He waved the sheet in his hand. "Caution, Tops. Something more could be afoot." Now he gave the note further attention. "Nothing about Karl Hermann in here, alas."

"If Scott's in Ben Ficklin, it's because he's still looking." Beneath the visor of his blue cap, Chance scanned the horizon thoughtfully. Was he thinking instead of Emma Neely, Davidson wondered.

"You stay on task, hear?" Davidson warned. "That's more than a raiding party out there. It's a fast-blowing heat wave."

"Better get started." Chance saluted, and turned on his heel toward the windswept grounds between here and the quartermaster's office.

As the sergeant left them, Davidson had an idea. He turned to the telegraph operator.

"Yessir?"

Davidson played with his whiskers once more. "I was just thinking about Scott Renald. At Ben Ficklin, he's less than a day's ride from Fort Concho and less than two days from Ox Creek. Talking Moon's his nephew, and he must still have some sway with the Comanche." He gestured toward the telegraph office. "Let's reply to Mr. Renald, shall we?"

Chapter Sixteen

The combatants all lay splayed on their backs in the shady thicket. Closest to Renald and Chivatá as they came upon the scene was Roy Danish, barely breathing. Blood coursed from his chest, maybe from his gut as well—too much blood. Beside him were his overturned hat and a relic repeater that drew a second, curious glance from Renald. A few paces away lay two warriors, side by side. One's head looked like a cracked egg. The other man was groaning, his moccasined heels working the soil, his hands clawing at an arrow embedded in his chest. His face was a scarred ruin. Somewhere to the left in a patch of grass was Bo's body, and in the scrub brush to the right, Reddy's. Beyond Reddy a cluster of three ponies grazed, one of them equipped with an especially large, empty bow slip. The slip caught Renald's eye.

Flies buzzed aplenty. The heavy air was beginning to stink.

"Dammit," Renald groaned as he squatted beside Danish, waving off the flies.

The wounded man rolled his head until his reddened eyes found Renald. "Apache bucks come outta them trees. I spun … done one." He raised his tremulous voice, straining to make sense of what had happened. "The ugly one got *arrow* shot. Reckon that."

Renald figured the man should depart knowing why. "You got between their business," he said. In a few more words, he recounted what had happened in Ben Ficklin, including Sam's part. All the while, his gaze combed the wood.

With effort, Danish replied, "I shoulda listened, stayed away."

"If you had, these braves would still be roaming free to kill others." It wasn't much, but it was all Renald could say to a man who'd given up his life for a couple of corpses.

A shadow crossed Renald's sightline; he could feel Danish flinch.

"That's my guide," he told him. Chivatá was making for the dying Apache.

Danish's shoulders seemed to settle on the porous ground. He nodded toward the wagon beside the river, struggling to get the words out. "Sam's first time out. Never brought … hides to market." With his eyelids shuttering down, he somehow managed a smile. "Gets everybody's shares now. Help him … with them hides … Cole Hawker, Fort Worth."

"Cole Hawker?" said Renald. "I know Hawk."

Danish looked pleased, for the last time. "He'll know what to do … Trappers' Rendezvous … too far, too much for Sam …"

"He'll be all right. Don't you worry."

Indeed, Roy Danish would never worry again. His chin came to rest near his wound. Renald laid a hand on his stiff shoulder.

Meanwhile, Chivatá rolled Burnt Face on his side to assess the depth of his wound. Slit-eyed, the man spotted Renald and coughed out a few words to her.

She rose straight up and trained her furious eyes on Renald. "He says it was *you* who threw him in the fire!"

At last, here it was—Renald's role in the Northern People massacre coming back to haunt him. Before responding, he made sure to breathe. "I wasn't leading the troop. Just trying to save those Hermann boys."

Chivatá edged away from the squirming warrior. "Who is next? The Lipan? The Mescalero? The Chiricahua?"

Renald lowered his gaze in reflection—and in some shame. For most of his years as a redeemer, he'd returned with a hostage and without ever firing a shot, but his career had ended in a bloodbath. Here was another one.

"I'll kill you," he heard her say.

Chivatá's waterlogged sidearm was as useless as his, but she also wore a blade. Sensing her greater chances, she reached for the knife.

Whether or not she really meant to use it, a bow twanged behind her, and with a crack of skin and flesh her arm went slack. She dropped to her knees, mouth agape.

Renald dipped down for Danish's rifle and spun toward Burnt Face, who was raising a short gun. Before either man could fire, another twang split the air and Burnt Face pitched back with a second arrow in his chest.

Throwing the gun down in disgust, Renald said, "No more bad luck for you …" Then, in the opposite direction, he cried out, *"Ashagoteh!"*—"Thanks!"

He turned back to Chivatá. She was clawing at her back, face pale with fear.

"I can do that," he said.

Coming forward, he saw Endah rise from behind some brush about twenty feet away. This first, solid view of Karl corrected Renald's impression of the boy. All along, despite the time elapsed and all the stories told about him, Renald had still recalled the adolescent of '74. Instead, this was a healthy European man's frame.

A man? He was sucking on a peppermint stick.

With Renald's attention arrested by Endah, Chivatá reached again for the blade, this time by jackknifing her good, left arm. But as the knife cleared the scabbard, Renald caught her wrist.

"Dumb," he scolded, twisting.

Forcing her to ease her grip, he seized the knife and tossed it out of reach. He sensed Endah's gaze following the throw. "You won't be needing this either," he said, taking Chivatá's six-gun.

He unfastened his belt and ripped it out, then held it toward her. "Bite down on it." Adjusting his position, he tore open the arrow's entry point in the cloth of her blouse. She tearfully chomped down on the leather strap while he dug his thumb and forefinger into the warm wound to access the arrowhead. A brief, careful yank followed, and he managed to extract the bloody object between his fingers. The wound wasn't particularly deep and didn't spurt. "Wedged into the muscle above the bone," he reported. "You're either very lucky or he just lobbed it."

He reclaimed his belt, then said, "Apply pressure while I get my kit."

She nodded with gritted teeth.

Rising, he cast a pointed glance at Endah, who was still sucking his candy. To her, Renald remarked, "A posse'll be looking for a store-dressed Indian. He best get back into whatever he was barely wearing."

Chivatá replaced her wince with a scowl. "The Apache wear clothes."

"He can't be too comfortable in a dead man's," he replied as he approached his horse.

Without waiting for a translation, the wide-framed but waffle-thick youth crossed Renald's path in the direction of the riverbank, wriggling out of his suspenders while offering the white man no more than a sideways acknowledgment.

When Renald returned with the kit and a whiskey bottle, Chivatá had wriggled out of her shirt and was shielding herself with her left arm crossed over her chest.

"Help yourself to this," he said, extending the whiskey. Shamefaced, she moved her good arm just enough to take it, while Renald kneeled to disinfect and dress her wound. Meantime, Endah located his native garments in the high grass. Wedging the mint stick between his teeth, the white Indian tore Bo's soggy clothes off himself and heaped them on the bare corpse from which they had come. After getting back into his own deerskin pants and long-sleeved tunic, he swept the grass with a moccasined foot, as if searching for something.

Renald kept a close eye on him before switching back to rip one of Chivatá's shirt sleeves off at the seam. Looping and knotting it under her wounded shoulder, he fashioned an improvised sling. She let him fit her injured arm into it. Suddenly he sensed movement from the direction of the riverbank. It was Endah striding forward, having claimed his discarded long bow and strapped his old quiver across his back.

Renald got to his feet. Endah stopped eye-to-eye with him, digging his bow into the ground and grasping the top end. Leaning on it, he said something.

"He asks what is next." This from a demoralized Chivatá, below.

Bending a knee, Renald responded, "I see. Now that near everybody who got mixed up in your flight is dead or wounded, it's time to just give yourself up!"

After a swig from the bottle, Chivatá translated. The youth merely shrugged.

"Well, you're right to fear a posse," Renald concluded.

Endah uttered something else in Apache. Renald thought he heard the word "Mason" in it.

"He says," she reported, "that he cannot promise he will return to Mason."

Renald scoffed. "You'd hang there. Not that you seem to care about your mother's feelings, but she's in Fort Worth with Freddie. Your father died of a broken heart."

Something of that clearly got through without a translation. The youth lowered his brow, a crease of mourning in it.

"Yeah, you think about that. Fortunately, he didn't live long enough to learn his firstborn takes scalps as a way of life." Renald put a hand on his irons. "I can make you a prisoner right now."

Endah replied sharply.

Renald didn't wait for Chivatá. He glared back at Endah. "That'll be the day! You deserve punishment for what you've done."

Endah answered again, still harsh, pretending to brush his hair with aggressive strokes.

"His father used the back of a hairbrush," Chivatá translated.

"Is that a suggestion?" Renald paused. Then he softened his tone. "Or is that why you never returned?"

Seeming to ignore him, Endah slung his bow over his shoulder, turned, and headed for the hunters' team of mules. Renald kept his revolver covered while Endah rummaged through the side bags. The youth returned with a man's folded shirt, maroon in color, and dropped it into Chivatá's lap.

Impressed, Renald kneeled to unbutton it. He draped it over Chivatá's bad shoulder and helped her slip her good arm into the left sleeve. Beneath the scrutiny of her close-in gaze, he buttoned her up. A break between her lips appeared, and behind it her white teeth gleamed. Then Endah, with almost apologetic awkwardness, tried to help her to her feet, but she shook him off. From her wobbly rise, it seemed the whiskey had done its work. Renald pried the bottle back from her.

Endah offered Chivatá his remaining mint stick. When she refused with a disgusted wave of her hand, he instead offered it to Renald.

"Don't mind if I do," he said.

A moment passed while both men savored their candies and Chivatá glowered from one to the other. Holding the mint stick between his teeth, Renald went to return the bottle and medical kit to his saddle bags. He came back to find Chivatá glaring at Endah.

"We could make Fort Concho before sundown," Renald told her. "You need a doctor. They've got an army surgeon there." He regarded Endah once more. The youth had stuck his great bow into the sand again, his right hand grasping the top bend, where the sinew met the nock. In his left hand, he held the candy to his lips. His brown eyes flashed thoughtfully.

"Did you understand me?" Renald asked him.

Out came the mint. *"Ein bisschen—doktor für Chivatá,* Fort Concho."

"They will send me to a reservation!" she protested.

"Like it or not, you've assisted an army redeemer," Renald countered. "I'll get you a pass back to the Kickapoo Springs when you're able."

"But I am Wichita through my mother."

"So?"

"I have no special bond to the Lipan. Besides, they are weak. I will join Caballero and Geronimo in New Mexico."

The words of a bruised warrior with some fight left in her. This might be important intelligence. Sketchy on matters Apache, Renald didn't really know. But he did know one leader from the other. "One's Mescalero, the other's Chiricahua. Why them?"

With some hesitation—and a hint of mourning—Chivatá said, "She was Mescalero."

"Who?" replied Renald. "You mean Nalen?"

"Do not speak her name."

"You loved her," he observed. To him, this merely meant sisterly love. "I'm sorry," he added.

"Again, your apologies tempt me to kill you," she replied.

"You really want to keep this going?"

"Or maybe I will kill somebody else. One white man is like another. The more dead palefaces, the better."

Renald shrugged in dismay. Whether he let her go now or later, she would put her freedom to ill use. How could he hold on to her, anyway? His hands were full with Karl. "Ever think," he said, "that half civilized and English-speaking, you're halfway there? I mean to living white. Since you're doomed to failure, maybe you should give it a try."

She averted her eyes, and while she looked away he raised the mint stick to his mouth.

Agitated voices began spilling across the South Concho. Men and horses were gathering on the opposite landing. The fellow Indian warriors exchanged wary looks.

"That didn't take long," said Renald.

Just then, they heard a call from across the river. "Renald! Scott Renald!"

Sensing Endah ready to start, Renald drew his six-gun at the youth. This creature could just as easily scamper off as cozy up now. "Don't," Renald cautioned.

The distant voice droned again. "Scott Renald! Roy Danish! Anybody over there?" It was a big voice that carried.

Renald pondered his options. At last he regarded Chivatá. "I'd be grateful if you don't stick a knife in my back."

Remote, expressionless, she merely held his gaze. Was that sufficient assurance?

Finally, she answered, "I will not help you anymore."

"Don't be so quick to resign your office," he responded. He gave a gunhawk's twirl of his weapon and holstered it. "I can protect you as my scout—from them."

He eyed Endah crosswise. "Come here," he said—simple words a German would understand. Surprisingly, Endah gestured as if he should lay down his bow. Renald restrained a smile. "*Nein*," he said. "But …" He tossed his own mint stick into the trees and whirled his finger to suggest Endah do likewise.

Endah savored a last lick before bidding farewell to this reminder of his white childhood.

Side by side, they stepped out of the trees.

* * *

Five men sat mounted across the water at an eighty-foot remove. Renald immediately recognized young Sam among them, this time fully clothed over his boots. Next to him was a stout older fellow in a fine suit. Beside the doctor was the apparent posse leader, likewise middle-aged, rougher dressed and balding, with broad shoulders. The bargemen were awaiting a signal to make the crossing.

Withdrawing something from beneath the lapel of his jacket, the posse leader again bridged the gap with his booming voice. "You Renald? Got a cable for you from Fort Richardson! Colonel says to rendezvous with Captain Norton and Talking Moon, Ox Creek supply point Sunday. You heard me right, that's Talking Moon of the Comanche!"

Talking Moon? Renald shook his head at his wily nephew's turn to play the white man's hero. *Play,* he repeated to himself.

"Been a breakout from Sill he's attempting to call back," the big man explained.

It had happened after all. Renald pictured what could follow: livestock stolen, settlers and skinners killed, captives taken. And by the feel of the warm southerly draft, the cavalry would have to scout thirsty. If the hostiles splintered, havoc could ensue all across western Texas. He shouted back, "It's safe to come over!"

The posse leader hesitated, cocking his head. "What's gone on over there? Where's Roy?"

"They're all dead," Renald responded. "Come see for yourself. Killed each other."

Even at a distance, young Sam's horror was unmistakable. He let out a whimper and wiped away the intrusion of tears.

The posse leader leaned over his horse's mane to prompt his men to follow him. Rewarded with enough nods, he spurred the animal downward into the river. The others followed, the barge pushing off behind them into the placid waters. Reaching the other side, the horses rose up in a cascading crash, their riders reacting with surprise at the skin color of the young warrior next to Renald.

"That brave's white!" snarled one of the young guns.

Renald met Sam's horse as it climbed onto the riverbank. Craning his neck, he established the facts hurriedly in a voice audible to all. "If it matters, Roy got one of the pair, this white brave the other." Then, to the group's leader, "I hope that disbands this posse."

"It plumb might," the big man grunted, swinging down with a screak of leather while scrutinizing the white warrior. The man was getting thick around the middle, but was still powerful-looking in the neck and shoulders under a weather-worn calfskin jacket.

Looking back at the wet-eyed Sam, Renald informed him of Roy Danish's last wishes concerning the haul. "It's all yours now," he told the youth. "I'll write you a letter of introduction to Cole Hawker."

The rest of the men dismounted and their leader shook Renald's hand vigorously, giving his name—"Ward O'Bannon, I run the livery—"and explaining his previous acquaintance with the ill-fated hunting party. "This here's Doc Thorndyke. Reckoned we might need a doc over here."

As the finely dressed Thorndyke stepped up belly first beside the rough-hewn O'Bannon, Renald replied that they could, in fact, use a doctor. He motioned toward the thicket, but was cut short by O'Bannon: "I heard about you, Renald. You was Army before the war. A civilian scout since?"

Renald clarified. "That's about right. This boy is Karl Hermann."

O'Bannon's form seemed to swell inside his jacket. The two young guns, emerging from between their horses, repeated Karl's name with seething disgust. "Scalping murderer!" one of them hissed.

Renald became conscious of Endah easing his right hand from the bow. He had no doubt the youth could loose an arrow as fast as any man among them could aim and fire his short gun. Endah would move fast, Renald imagined, leaping to one side, and three men would go down before he vanished into the trees. Urgently, Renald raised his voice. "Make no mistake, I'm returning Karl to his mother."

"I heard you was waving around a commission in town," said O'Bannon.

Renald withdrew the folded sheet from his breast pocket while O'Bannon fumbled in his own pocket to produce the cable from Colonel Davidson. They exchanged documents, and Renald read Davidson's hunch that Cedar Lake and Farther Lake were likely stops on the breakouts' path. He pondered the recommendation, unconvinced.

"Lookie here!" O'Bannon exclaimed to all. "We got no less than *two* legends among us! Why, this here's Scott Renald! Ever heard of the Survivor's Bluff Massacre? They say he took on a whole Tonk war party! Slaughtered 'em to a man and killed the chief."

Renald, fearing that knife in his back from the unseen third legend present, said, "What I did was for Laura Little and her son. Cole Hawker saved us both. Speaking of Indians, Doc, my scout could use your attention." He gestured toward the interior. "Got herself injured in the action."

Thorndyke sucked in his gut. "A squaw, you say?"

"I'd sure appreciate it." Renald threw a glance behind him to check on Chivatá.

But she was gone—and so, they shortly discovered, was a sidearm and one of the dead braves' ponies. Renald marveled that she had mounted a padded horse one-handed and with a fair amount of whiskey in her. Bound for the renegades in New Mexico Territory?

The next twelve to fifteen hours would decide her fate. If no fever ensued and she kept the wound clean, she could go a long way indeed. Facing the shadowy thicket, Renald found himself hoping they'd meet again. When he turned to the men, his gaze touched on Endah, leaning on his oversized bow. Behind the youth, the sun-drenched river area formed a vivid, promising backdrop.

"Anybody here speak German?" Renald asked.

* * *

When Endah saw Chivatá reach for her blade, his reaction would prove fateful for everybody. No sooner had the redoubtable Chivatá fallen to her knees than Endah realized he'd made the unimaginable possible: now, any option other than sticking close to the white man was fraught with greater peril. With palefaces on his heels, could he manage to make it past Fort Concho? Fighting thirst, could he locate the Comanche on the Llano in time? If he got that far, would they accept him as a fellow Indian refugee? Or could he somehow reach the Apache or Ghost Mountains instead?

Best to stick with this paleface.

He recognized the man who'd rescued his brother and thrown Burnt Face into the fire. He remembered the event as if it were yesterday. If only for the space of a breath, Endah became his old self again when he drew on Chivatá to protect Freddie's rescuer, though the thought of actually becoming white again never crossed his mind.

Now, with his longbow dug into the ground and both hands gripping the upper limb, he watched the unfolding scene with a boy's curiosity. To his right, the wide-open river area glittered and gloried, while to his left the shadowy interior simply sulked. Next to the rig, heaped with skins, a vigorous dispute was playing out between the men from town. For the time being they had well forgotten him. Two of the younger members of the posse, facing off against their elders, were engaged in a combination of spitting, cussing, and boot stomping. The pair of elders—Fine Clothes Man and Big Man—both indulged them with a tolerance surprising to Endah.

And then there was the distraught Straw Hair sitting off to the side. This boy, apparently, was good for nothing except crying, rocking, and clutching his midsection, as if at any second he would either keel over in pain or lose control of his bowels. His state of helplessness reminded Endah of his own brother following their capture. Chin-tie stood between the opposing factions with his arms crossed.

During the youngers' verbal onslaught, Fine Clothes Man suddenly raised a hand and said something that caused Big Man to nod his head with shut eyes. Finally, Chin-tie broke in and spoke at length in an insistent tone. Next, shaking their heads, the young pair broke off and started dragging the white men's bodies onto the barge. During this process—and of much amusement to Endah—Straw Hair curled up and wept, causing Fine Clothes Man to bend down and offer him a folded white cloth, which the boy used to dry his eyes. Meantime, Chin-tie and Big Man occupied themselves with rounding up the animals, beginning with the two dead white men's horses, including the one Endah had rustled in town. The barge operators collected the long gun Roy Danish had carried over.

The barge crossed the river with the white dead, then returned for their rig. Only when it came back did Endah understand what the debate had been about. The operators brought two spades with them, which Chin-tie and Big Man promptly took off their hands. Without pause the pair set to digging graves for the dead Northern People while everybody else sat and watched, bemused.

Then Chin-tie called to him.

Using clumsy hand signals, the paleface told him to arrange the bodies in the shallow holes. This prompted a contemptuous scowl from Big Man, till now agreeable. He promptly lumbered off with his spade. Chin-tie followed in Big Man's tracks to join the rest, his abandoned tool protruding from the ground.

As he dragged Burnt Face's body over to one of the pits, Endah's admiration and affinity for Chin-tie grew. The graves had been dug according to custom, from east to west, allowing him to point his fellow Apaches' moccasins toward the sunset. By contrast, an Apache or any Indian would've simply left his victims—white or otherwise—to bloat and rot. And if time permitted, they would've defiled the corpses with glee. To an Indian, the enemy wasn't human. Chin-tie was different. *He is better than any of us*, thought Endah, *and better than any other white man too.*

He yanked the arrow from Burnt Face's chest.

Before covering the body, Endah allowed himself a prize: Burnt Face's tasseled and beaded knife slip. But he put the weapon itself in the dead man's hands crossed on his chest, to honor his courage.

Endah would later fill the sheath with Chivatá's lost blade.

* * *

Renald, having found a stable writing surface between O'Bannon's rounded shoulder blades, completed his signature with a flourish—a sliding "d" to be exact—quite at odds with his reserved nature. He handed Sam the note. "That'll get you in to see Cole Hawker at the Big C-H."

Released, O'Bannon set himself in motion toward his men, who were occupied with stabilizing the buckboard on the raft. Folding the sheet, Sam noticed printed lines on the obverse side.

"What's this?" he asked, scrutinizing it:

Authorized Redeemer ________________
Date _________________________
Tribe ________________________
Name of Captive (Indian) ___________
Birth name (if known) ______________
Transaction amount in $ ____________
Additional trade items ______________
Name Indian releaser ______________
Signature (or mark) _______________
Redeemer signature _______________

Transaction amount payable or redeemable in cash or goods equivalent for six months from date of issuance at any U.S. Army post by order of Office of Secretary of Army with Office of Indian Affairs.

"That's what's called a redemption coupon," said Renald. Nodding in Endah's direction, he added, "Don't have to use one for him, though."

The Indian youth was reclining with his back against a tree just a few paces away, looking perfectly bored. Never mind that he'd just killed a man and shot a woman, and before that killed a pony and sent a whole town into a panic.

"What'dya think he'll do?" asked Sam, his eyes finally dry. "Just ride into Fort Worth with you?"

"The nearest post is where I gotta leave him. And Concho happens to be smack on the way to Ox Creek."

"He could run anytime, 'specially if you let him have his weapon."

"I'm hoping that as long as I let him keep it," replied Renald, "he'll ride this horse in the direction it's going—if you get my meaning."

"Back to his family?"

"Back to his mother and his brother. It's a hard call to ignore when it finally reaches you." He snapped his fingers. "It signals the end of the adventure—for a lad his age, that is. Doesn't mean it's easy adjusting. It sure ain't."

Nodding toward Endah, Sam said, "Wish I could be there when his mother sees him again."

Renald appraised Endah in response. "Sometimes, when the kid is taken real young and returned way later, even his own parents don't recognize him, can't even communicate. But beneath the long hair and browned skin, there's something left of Karl Hermann."

"All set!" cried one of the flatboat operators from the river bank. The buckboard wagon was now secured on the craft. The pair of young guns led the saddled horses there, while O'Bannon and Thorndyke moved purposefully toward Renald.

"We'll be rounding up them ponies next," O'Bannon announced. Stopping before Renald in a patch of light, he added, "We should get something outta this, don't you think?"

Renald didn't care to respond.

"Pleased to have met you, Mister Renald," the doc told him. He gestured toward the fresh burial mounds. "Appreciated your supporting me on that."

"It wasn't just for the hygiene," Renald answered.

With that, he offered help gathering the Indian ponies. "You're gonna spook 'em if you try it yourselves." He whistled, gaining Endah's attention, then made the necessary hand signals.

As the boy got to his feet, O'Bannon remarked, "Already got him tamed, I see."

Watching Endah rounding up the ponies, Renald responded, "Beauty is, it's his choice. You'll fetch a nice price for those two ponies."

"Two?" replied O'Bannon. "I see *three* there."

Renald asked, "Do you expect him to walk?"

"A mule will do for *him*," O'Bannon protested. "He's a prisoner, ain't he?"

"Is he?"

"You think you can trust 'im, arrows 'n' all?"

"My having redeemed his brother counts for something, I reckon."

O'Bannon fixed Renald with a grave, level-eyed look—one meant to sober him up. "You got a tiger by the tail there, mister," O'Bannon cautioned. "Young Sam tells me you're headed to Fort Concho with him. I'll wire ahead just in case you make it."

For his part, Doc Thorndyke wholeheartedly wished Renald luck, adding with an ear-to-ear smile, "To you both, that is."

Part IV

Lost at Lost Lake

Chapter Seventeen

The way north began with Renald and Endah crossing the river behind the others, and then heading north up the army road toward Fort Concho, half a day's ride with walking rest. The road lay on the open west side for a reason. Lining the eastern bank was a thicket of soaring cottonwoods, expansive madrones, and brambles of juniper and sage—a tantalizing sight for two men baking in the sun. Sweat was the price for speed. From the unseasonably hot draft in their faces, they experienced something of the conditions affecting the Llano ahead, and the brown channel of water was little inducement to cool off. The dawn beef drive had left cattle droppings dotting the path.

While riding side by side with his new companion, Renald occasionally offered Endah a drink of water, and the warrior partook sparingly before handing back the canteen. Lacking a shared language, and because riding abreast made signing awkward, most of their journey was spent in inward reflection.

To Renald, Endah seemed almost impossibly levelheaded, but behind the warrior's cool veneer was a tortured soul.

Endah was feeling the grief of a son whose father had been murdered, the sorrow of an orphan who had killed his own lover in revenge. Pity he felt for Chivatá, whom he'd humiliated and sent into flight. He even felt sorry for the hapless Burnt Face and his brother; and he felt ashamed that Chief Tall Grass had lost two more men. Finally, he felt a queasy uncertainty about the future—for he guessed that the deep-down truth about himself, unlocked in the Lipan camp, could not be accepted in the direction he was heading.

Meantime, Scott Renald was thinking less about the welfare of 10th Troop, and more about the two strong women who'd entered his life of late. Each was endowed with admirable character and determination, and yet each was a case of loss and unfulfillment. Chivatá, the irrepressible rebel, was a haunted fighter hopelessly unable to win, while the scarred Trude Hermann was a widowed mother ever soldiering on. Renald found himself alternating between thoughts about Chivatá and thoughts about Trude—both spirited, admirable women—as if he must choose between them.

Admittedly, when Chivatá vanished into the wood, he felt something leave him in her flight—a faint hope of more? Yes, it had been there, this feeling, this fantasy. But with Chivatá gone, and perhaps destined for a feverish death—or perhaps lost to Caballero and Geronimo and another sorry fate—his daydream settled on Trude Hermann, a far more likely match if he were to see a woman in his future. He glanced sidelong at Endah, riding his pony unawares. Could making him Karl again be their mutual endeavor? Renald casually noted the boy's flowing hair, his strikingly grandiose bow, the stuffed quiver. Then, as he called up the image of Karl's mother, she wasn't clothed in the verdant dress she'd worn to Martha's;

neither was she wearing face-paint. Instead Renald saw Trude in her plain housedress at the door of her apartment. It was the unadorned Trude that appealed to this stark Plains trooper. In his memory a blush raised her hollow cheeks.

Renald's thoughts were interrupted when Endah leapt suddenly from his pony, hit the ground in a crouch, and loosed an arrow that caught a stray calf in the neck. As the animal collapsed, kicking and bellowing and spurting blood, Endah was already upon it with Chivatá's knife. The beast suffered for mere seconds before the Indian dispatched it and sliced open its belly. Renald looked on in amazement as the youth dug his hands in, tore out the stomach and the organs attached to it, and—with quick cuts—separated them from the esophagus at one end and the intestines at the other. Then, sucking from the esophagus stump, he guzzled mother's milk, some spilling down his chin. Next, he separated the liver—or was it the pancreas?— with an expert slash, and fed himself with it from both hands. In less than a minute he finished lunch, then rinsed his hands and face in the river, and was back on his pony.

Renald told him, "Shame on you for not sharing."

* * *

On the river's south bank, across from the town of Saint Angela, the lodgepole walls of Fort Concho were misleadingly impressive. Today the post was all but empty. Entering through the swung-open gate after a guard's approving cry, Renald was met with a bleakness that bespoke the thinned ranks there. Absolutely nobody was about except those manning the gate, or so it seemed at first glance. In actual fact, just sixteen men had stayed behind when Norton marched out with his meager force. As Renald had worked out of Fort Concho when assigned to the 4th Cavalry, he knew in which direction to swing his horse. He wondered who he would find in the C.O.'s office.

A lone officer greeted them in front of the steps—his white skin revealing relatively high rank from a distance. Behind him, a black trooper in a private's cap was standing outside the door. Renald stepped down while Endah remained on his horse. The officer's voice boomed in drill sergeant fashion. "So! You are the famous Scott Renald! I am Lieutenant Schmidt."

"Schmidt?" replied Renald with real excitement. "Oh, thank God—a German speaker!"

Behind the imposing Schmidt, the lanky private folded his arms.

"I take it you're a holdover from Colonel Grierson's command," said Renald.

"Captain Norton is understrength. Some troops have deployed to the Rio Grande, others gone to escort Colonel Davidson to Fort Custer. It is a *great* pleasure to meet you, Mr. Renald."

Relieved to be able to offload Karl, Renald replied, "I assure you, Lieutenant, the pleasure is all mine—this here is Karl Hermann. All yours!"

"Good one, Mr. Renald! Colonel Davidson sent a wire to expect you, but he did *not* mention Herr Hermann." He flashed a curious look at the white Apache. "*Wie geht es dir?*"

"*Danke, gut,*" Endah grunted.

Turning back to Renald, Schmidt said, "This boy has *blood* on his sleeves!"

Renald sighed. "Don't ask …"

Schmidt nodded. "Well, I'm sure you have all under control."

"When does the next coach get in?"

A touch of confusion showed on Schmidt's features. "Not till Wednesday …"

Renald chose a phrase almost surely incomprehensible to Endah. He nodded toward the youth. "Got accommodations for him till then?"

Schmidt answered heartily. "No drunks in the guardhouse— all on scout!" He leaned forward. "But is he dangerous?"

"Ask him."

"Yes, let us ask," said Schmidt. *"Bist du eine Gefahr für mich?"*

The youth shook his head.

With a hopeful tinge in his voice, Renald added, "Ask him if he wants to sleep on a bed for the first time in years."

But this English, the white warrior understood. *"Nein,"* he responded sharply.

"Big fella!" the lieutenant observed, hauling back. "Just look at them shoulders. *German* shoulders! You redeemed his brother, yes?"

Renald nodded. "I assisted Sergeant Chance. Is he riding with Norton?"

"Sergeant Chance is en route from Fort Richardson to Ox Creek. Them hostiles took *fifty* horses from Fort Sill and hit a buffalo hunter camp. A man butchered, horses took, who knows what else." Schmidt looked glum. "Captain Norton has only thirty men."

"I'd like to see Ox Creek on the map."

"Come in and I will show you. *Kaffee?*"

"I prefer coffee," said Renald.

With an amused grin, Schmidt slapped his arm. "Perhaps the boy likes coffee too? *Trinkst du Kaffee?*"

"*Natürlich!*" Endah alighted from his horse and began to pull his bow from its slip. Did he really think he might need it?

"*Es ist verboten, deine Waffe mitzunehmen,*" Schmidt told him. "It is forbidden to bring your weapons inside." Renald watched with wonder as Endah readily accepted Schmidt's authority and let the bow slip back into its tasseled boot. Turning toward Renald, Schmidt remarked, "From the size of it, I would say fairy tales from the old country he remembers. Not a practical weapon on horseback, though."

Renald scratched the side of his nose. "He's plenty good on foot."

"Then he must be completely disarmed!" Schmidt flapped his fingers and nodded toward Endah's knife. Obediently, Endah handed it hilt-first to Schmidt, who turned and sank it into the timber of the entrance H-frame.

Schmidt reverted to his orderly. "A pot of *kaffee*. And alert the cook!"

The young private seemed resentful of the order. Passing Renald, he sneered, "Johnny Reb Renald …"

It was a typical slight against Scott Renald coming from a member of the 10th, and this time Sergeant Chance was not around to run interference between him and the black troopers. Renald left it unanswered.

* * *

Some minutes later, the three men were hunched over Colonel Grierson's desk, backs to the door, examining a location map of the southeast corner of the Llano Estacado, or the "Yarner," as some called it. Amber lamplight compensated for the greying glow cast by a few cloudy windows. Situated in the middle, Renald was still wearing his hat, tied under his chin and pushed back. Wisps of white hair rested on his sun-browned forehead. To his right hulked Endah. To his left, Schmidt was pointing at a spot on the map and talking at a decibel too high for indoors.

"Here is the supply base, at the bend of Ox Creek." His finger moved west on the map from Ox Creek to Cedar Lake, then further west to an ink oval representing Farther Lake. With a commander's authority, he said, "We think the breakouts will travel between these waterholes to meet the resident Yarner bands." In Schmidt's accent, *Yarner* sounded like "Yanah."

Just then, his orderly entered, carrying a tray that bore a kettle and three rattling cups.

Schmidt rapped a free area on the desk with his knuckles. "And why not *four* cups?"

"Bad enough, I gotta serve 'im," replied the mere private, for Renald's ears. "Can't expect me to sip coffee with him none." With that, he stepped off to the side and folded his arms.

Renald told him he understood.

"Do you now, Johnny Reb Renald?"

Schmidt shrugged and poured the coffee himself, his orderly observing them tersely. He held out a steaming cup to the former captain before serving Endah. The smell of fresh coffee was most welcoming. Renald took a sip, not failing to notice how comical his white Indian companion looked holding a porcelain coffee cup.

"As I was saying …" Schmidt tapped a place on the map.

"*Nein,*" Endah chirped.

Renald, jerking his coffee cup involuntarily, scalded his lips.

The white warrior conveyed something to Schmidt in their common language. Schmidt shifted his view to Renald. "Says he was there recently to trade. Cedar Lake was dry."

"Already?" replied Renald. He squeezed his lips together against the burn.

"Somewhere else he found Comanches. And they were expecting the breakouts."

Now Endah indicated a location north and *east*. "*Hier waren sie.*"

"Rich Lake," Schmidt read aloud.

Renald fretted, brow creased. "A stone's throw from Ox Creek," he muttered. Gripping the rim of his cup as if it were that very stone, he bent a knee. "With as much horse flesh as the Comanche have, they'll cut across the terrain like the wind—even with women and children. Their purpose is not to hunt buffalo but to evade detection—so it's doubtful they'll follow any known route. Rather than making a circuit of the lakes to absorb other bands, they'll get word to them somehow. I always marveled at how Indians could find each other out there. Now, judging by the oven-hot draft we faced on our ride from Ben Ficklin, it's drought conditions on the Llano. Norton can't haul water around with him, so it's a dangerous situation as he looks for their trail ever further west."

Schmidt nodded vigorously. "I see now why Colonel Davidson wanted your help."

"Norton needs to know," said Renald. "If we don't catch him in time, he's gonna get real thirsty on that scout."

"Maybe Talking Moon has better intelligence," said Schmidt hopefully.

"That's just what I'm afraid of." Renald raised an eyebrow of suspicion at Endah. "I'd trust this kid here over my own nephew. Lieutenant, could you send a galloper ahead with Karl's information?"

"They's all with Captain Norton. But such a distance Talking Moon could not cover by morning."

"He's a former raider, not a cavalry unit. Never underestimate an Indian on a horse."

"My available men are recruits, not scouts."

Renald eyed the haughty private, still observing wordlessly. "Then let's keep the babes safe behind these walls," he said. "I better take a barrel of water with me in case that creek has dried up."

"Captain Norton has all the four-wheelers. Of course, some will come back for more supplies."

"Can't wait for that." Renald stepped out from between the two men and motioned toward Endah. "Maybe *he* can be useful. You got some extra canteens?"

Schmidt nodded, divining Renald's intention. "Got plenty of empty powder cans too."

"Good. And a couple of mules for each of us? Fine." He turned to Endah. "I could use your help."

The lieutenant explained in German, only to elicit a biting reply from the warrior. Shrugging, Schmidt reported, "He asks why he should help the palefaces."

"Palefaces?" Renald regarded the black orderly. "Does he look pale to you?"

Endah said something in reply.

Schmidt translated. "Still, they are Army. Why should he help the army?"

Endah sipped his coffee.

This was too much for Renald. He restrained the urge to knock the cup from the boy's grasp. Instead he replied,

"Because it's those same Negroes who risked their lives for you and Freddie. Remember? The same that brought your brother back to your brokenhearted parents."

The black private began to look at Renald differently—Renald sensed it. Was Endah softening as well? He continued. "Three years with the Apache can't make that disappear, can it? You felt beholden to *me,* so why not to them?"

Endah lowered his chin. At last he met Renald's gaze. "I stay with you," he said.

Naturally, thought Renald—back on the trail, Endah's options remained. "Make no mistake," he responded. "I need a *willing* partner, not somebody I gotta cover with my gun."

After Endah offered a brief response in German, Schmidt translated. "For what it's worth, his promise you got …"

Renald scoffed. "If only it were a *German's* promise." He set his cup on the tray. "What we'll lose in time using mules instead of wheels, we'll gain in mobility in case we need it."

As it happened, they would need just that.

Chapter Eighteen

As dusk began to settle onto the cooling tablelands, Trooper Tyler, picketed southeast of camp in a rocky outcrop, noticed something out there. At a remove of about half a mile, a fast-moving speck could only be taken for a lone rider. A galloper sent from Fort Concho? Couldn't be. All had gone with Norton. He pulled his binoculars and peered out again from the stones concealing him. Behind him, his charger bobbed its head and stamped a hoof.

"I hear him too …" Tyler muttered. "He's trying to beat darkness and heading straight for the depot."

Tyler was quite accustomed to talking to his horse. In fact, he talked more to his horse than to anybody. "Can't just ride headlong into him," he observed.

Dusting his uniform's yellow-piped calves, he rose. His job wasn't to engage with hostiles, but to report on them. Yet this was just a single rider, and while unthreatening enough, making contact meant exposing the army's presence out here. With a huff, Tyler slipped the field glasses into their case on his saddle. He drummed his gloved fingers on the seat a moment, then pivoted back to the stone window, framing the outside movement. The rider, circumventing Tyler's refuge at a rapid clip, began to bank southward, his mount durable but far from fresh. Tyler and his rested horse could easily overtake them.

He looked his own animal in the eye. "Ready for some action, sweetie? Damned if it ain't been a while."

With that he swung up, reining his horse toward the jagged exit.

There they paused, and Tyler cast his view over the still and darker flatlands to the west. Wind whistled through gaps in the stone walls, and somewhere a coyote cried. After a minute or so, the rider appeared again, plunging westward like a slow-moving bullet bound for 10th Troop. A curious thing indeed.

Finally, Tyler chirruped his animal. "Let's go—yippie!"

A double-heeled kick launched their charge, and they exploded from the rugged place.

In under a minute Tyler, sidearm drawn and pointing skyward, was coming up behind his target. The black hair, restrained by a distinct headband, identified the rider as Apache—and an almost coy turn of the cheek corrected Tyler's assumption this was a man. Registering her pursuer, she pulled back, and even before her mount came to a halt she'd leapt from its back, landing on both buckskin boots with hardly a bend of the knees. She wore an oversized maroon shirt, her right arm in a sling.

Hauling back on the reins, Tyler holstered his gun in a cloud of dust.

"I am Chivatá," she told him at once.

He dismounted, breathlessly. Here was the storied woman warrior of the Lipan Apache. One of them. He glanced around as if looking for someone else. "If you're Chivatá, where's Nalen?"

Her long-lashed eyes narrowed. "Do not speak her name."

He understood. The Apache did not utter the names of the dead. "That explains the chopped hair," he said.

Sweat glistened on her brow, and she seemed slightly unsteady on her feet. Tyler also noticed the gunsling strapped to her shapely hips. Her revolver was ensconced in its holster butt-out to enable a left-handed draw across the body. He could draw faster, he told himself. On her belt she wore an empty knife slip.

"Want to tell me what happened?" He indicated her bound arm.

She answered matter-of-factly. "Karl Hermann shot me in the back."

"Karl Hermann?" Tyler's voice cracked at the surprise. "That how you lost your knife too?"

"We found him near a town south of Fort Concho."

"That'd be Ben Ficklin. Who's *we*? You and—?"

"Me and Scott Renald."

"Renald?" *Damn*, he thought—*but keep your guard up.* "Ain't he retired?"

"If that was true, I would not be riding alone."

What a story was unfolding. But it didn't add up yet. "And yet you partnered with him to find the Hermann boy?"

"Punishment," she explained. "Chief Tall Grass was angry we attacked Renald."

"If you attacked Renald," he said, "how come *we's* talking like old friends?"

"I will tell you as we ride."

Her comportment was remarkable. But she appeared spent. She needed the army sawbones.

"Ride? To where?"

"To *Capitán* Norton at Ox Creek, of course."

So coolly did she state her intentions, and with such startling knowledge of the troop's position, that Tyler leaned back as if blown by a random gust. "Ox Creek?"

"Do not play stupid. Sergeant?"

"Tyler. Sergeant Tyler."

"I will explain as we ride, Sergeant Tyler. There is little time."

"Looks to me like you and your pony need a rest first."

"Your command must know."

He cocked his head, feeling the night chill. "Must know what?"

Her chin rose. "I know you are here to find the Comanche raiders, and that Talking Moon will meet you at Ox Creek. But I do not report to sergeants. Take me to *Capitán* Norton. I give you my gun." She showed him the thumb and index finger of her left hand before she pulled the sidearm from her waist.

Accepting the dangled weapon by the handle, Tyler patted his own saddle seat. "Some walking rest for your mount? I'll even help you up on mine."

With a tinge of the South in her voice, she responded, "What a gentleman …"

* * *

Later, in the army surgeon's tent, Chivatá lay cheek-to-mat on the operating table, tautened skin defining her face, shoulders exposed above a woolen blanket. Trooper Tyler sat on a stool opposite. To his right, the raven-bearded and blue-eyed Captain Norton, tall from the hips up, hunched on his seat, hands clasped between the knees of his service pants. Tyler sensed his tension. Norton wasn't worried about Chivatá's condition— he was divided over what to do with the information she'd delivered. Seated to Norton's right was the equally concerned Sergeant Chance.

By the light of a hanging lamp the bearded doctor was beginning his work on the prostrate woman, his animated shadow playing on the door flap to the left. The canvas behind them billowed and rested from the night draft.

"Just what have you got wedged in here?" he asked, patting the spot with a cotton wedge. "Dung of some sort?"

"That word I do not know," she said. "It is of the horse."

Over her, he glanced at the others. "A novel definition of a clean wound! Let's try some good ol' disinfectant, shall we? This'll hurt some."

She stiffened, visibly. "I am not afraid."

"It's no deeper than the arrowhead that made it," said the doc, doing his work while she winced. "Forty-eight hours and you'll be back to … whatever you were doing. Damned lucky, I'd say." He pinched the runny gash shut. "It's as if he didn't want to hurt you too bad."

"You are hurting me more!"

Unheeding, the sawbones told her, "Stitches and a tight wrap is all you need, provided you rest." Then to Norton, "I recommend she recuperates here a few days."

"No!" She raised her head. "You need me."

"Need you?" Norton asked. "What for?"

"Across the border," she replied.

"May we proceed?" The doctor pushed her head back down with one hand while accepting a needle and thread from his uniformed male assistant with the other.

The wind outside bellowed.

Chivatá had just finished reporting to Norton that, following a coordinated plan, the Comanche breakouts would by now have splintered off from their women and children. While their families were still destined with their plunder for a secret encampment at Farther Lake, the men intended to unite with Caballero and Geronimo in New Mexico after massing with still more renegades at the distant Lost Lake. A surprise assault on the 9th Cavalry of buffalo soldiers at Fort Stanton was imminent. Although Texas-wide, pan-tribal mayhem had been anticipated by all, nobody in the ranks had dreamt up this unfolding catastrophe, and there was no telegraph line nearby to transmit an alarm.

Rising, Norton confessed, "The borderlands are beyond the range of my scouts' knowledge." He gave Chivatá a hard look. "I take it you have that knowledge," he said.

"I do," she replied.

Sergeant Chance was about to react when his commander stopped him with a raised hand. "We'll conference outside, Tops. Come along, Tyler."

The three men stepped out and proceeded a distance from the tent. Around them on the cracked desert turf were smaller trooper tents arranged in rows, and here and there campfires blazed with men lounging around them. A typical start to a dry country scout, before the heat of the day and the cold of the night sank in, before the liquor ran out. One group, the de facto chorus of the command, was singing spirituals to pass the time, just one hymn of many to be heard on a given day. A man felt warm and safe here, despite the adversity of the environment and its native inhabitants. At least he could be reasonably confident that no attack would be made on such a force, particularly at night. But all three men shared a nagging concern: were their two stripped-down companies enough for the job?

"Tops," said Norton to Chance, "sounds like a wee bit o' drink is making the rounds. See to it the men go easy. No telling where we'll find the next waterhole." He turned to Tyler. "I need my fastest runner for this. Tomorrow you'll return to Fort Concho and give a full report for the wire. Tell Lieutenant Schmidt we couldn't wait for Talking Moon, but are leaving instructions for his party to proceed alone to Farther Lake for the squaws and children. Caution Schmidt to be on his guard. Fort Stanton could be a diversion and Fort Concho the real target."

To Tyler, this was an obvious ploy on Norton's part to avoid sharing credit with Talking Moon and the colonel—Mackenzie—who had dispatched him. Nevertheless, if Chivatá was to be believed, the troop should indeed get a move on. Though he could be faulted for self-interest, and on one previous scout for lacking resolve, Norton was on balance a decisive commander who admirably exercised both boldness and caution.

"From Concho," Norton continued, "report back here to await our location. I don't want you riding around in a heat wave looking for us."

Tyler frowned his disapproval.

"Get some shuteye, trooper. We're all gonna need a few hours tonight." Norton turned again to Tops. "You had something to say?"

Chance cleared his throat. "Respectfully, sir, we didn't ask the squaw to produce a note from Renald, and she ain't offered none."

"She's wounded, isn't she? Wounded by another Indian no less. She's acquainted with Renald's mission, and she has knowledge of the breakout …"

Chance's thin mustache drooped with his downturned lips. "Seems so, sir," he conceded.

"And she informs us that Davidson traded cables with Renald in Ben Ficklin, which means she was with Renald when he sent that cable that you saw for yourself. Then she shows up here. So, why shouldn't we take her at her word?" Norton regarded Tyler. "An army redeemer would head to the nearest post with his prize, so I expect you'll find Scott Renald at Fort Concho waiting for the Wednesday stage to set Karl Hermann on. You can check her story with him."

"Yessir."

"I know enough to act on," Norton said, as if to himself. "To not act would be …" He left the sentence dangling, interrupted by an unexpected commotion at the edge of camp.

In his head, Tyler completed Norton's thought: *to abstain from action would be "cowardly."*

Men's voices began to bellow from a distance, and Tyler read disappointment on Norton's face. "Talking Moon," echoed the captain.

"You will need an interpreter." It was Chivatá, wrapped in her blanket, whisking past them. The three officers followed after her—as the entire troop would do the next day.

Chapter Nineteen

From the outset, Sergeant Chance had his doubts about sending the troop deep into the desert in the middle of a drought, toward a fixed destination set by an unreliable source—as any random Indian was until proven otherwise. Yet, recalling Davidson's counsel, he'd suppressed his inclination to protest Norton's judgment in this regard: their mutual commander had, after all, cautioned not to lay chase. The Comanche were adept at creating either remarkably convincing diversionary trails or genuine ones that could vanish on hard ground, leaving even the best Tonk scout scratching his head. Instead, Davidson had advised they seek out the renegades' waterholes, and that was just what Norton was determined to do, albeit by listening to the potentially dubious Chivatá. But Norton was an able commander, and while he agreed to follow her beyond the New Mexico border, the plan was to divert northwest toward Lost Lake only after first checking if the breakouts had been through Cedar Lake.

Reached near dusk on Day Two, Cedar Lake bore no trace of recent Indian presence, however—and it was unseasonably dry.

Fortunately for the troop, by digging holes deep into its bed the soldiers were able to rehydrate for the first time. Observing this activity, Sergeant Chance noticed the men's frantic behavior as they thrust their tin cups and canteens downward in a tangle of arms and wrists to get no more than sandy, saline refreshment for it. Yet the ability to dig successfully for water in a dry lake helped lessen the troopers' fears. It also reinforced Norton's plan to continue the scout northwest the following day.

As for Farther Lake, where Chivatá had said they would find the women and children, Norton stuck to his plan of sending Talking Moon and his delegation of five there. Less than a year after the Little Big Horn disaster, he was understandably reluctant to divide the troop. And he was equally eager to rid himself of Talking Moon. Let the Indian chase the women and children.

* * *

Day Three began at dawn as Talking Moon departed for Farther Lake, while the troop, with Chivatá scouting ahead—her sidearm restored—started for Lost Lake. By eight a.m., the men were already swallowing hot air and wiping sweat from their brows. A small stain had appeared on the back of Norton's shirt, between his suspenders. From many previous summer scouts together, Sergeant Chance knew that Norton could take the heat better than most men. To a degree, the Irishman even enjoyed it—as only a man from a grim country could. But every man had his limits, and a desert drought could drive even the hardiest trooper to them between sunrise and sundown. As Chance rode behind his superior officer at the head of the column, he prayed under his breath they wouldn't become beef jerky on this scout. Short of finding satisfactory water somewhere, a crisis was inevitable.

Unavoidably, Chance thought of his wife and two girls at Fort Richardson—and of what he must endure before he would reunite with them, regardless of any action seen. Each parched step northwest would have its thirstier equivalent on their march back. He licked his sere lips. At least he had a wife to think of, a love to long for. By contrast, Norton was a fresh widower whose two young children were in the care of another army wife. Chance mustn't forget what a suffering man Norton was.

His thoughts also touched on Emma Neely, that little girl taken from his friends at Old Fort Chadbourne. Scolding himself, he regretted not informing Talking Moon of her disappearance. He should've thought ahead to the promise of Farther Lake. Perhaps, if the Comanche women were found there, united with others from the Llano, she might be there too. He pursed his lips at the oversight—he hadn't mentioned Emma to Chivatá either. Such had been his haste to ready the men for a difficult scout.

Such was his commander's stubbornness that they were still on it.

A man's mind is prone to wandering on a monotonous desert march, but increasing temperatures and lengthening exposures inevitably set him straight. Chance craned his neck and squinted up at the cruel, blistering orb, the sight of which instantly dispersed his musings like a stone tossed into a flock of birds. His thoughts, each and every one of them, must be devoted to the survival of his men.

Emma Neely must not interfere.

* * *

Not a single head of buffalo or pronghorn was glimpsed all morning, nor a wisp of cloud, and though they passed without difficulty through vast areas of switchgrass and grama as high as a horse's belly, their animals complained in other parts dominated by sharp daggergrass. As the day wore on, Norton's sweat stain grew until it occupied most of the stalwart captain's back, while on Chance's own sticky backside he could feel his men's forlorn, questioning eyes. Their hush on the march was telling. No singing this day, no fraternal joking. Just creaking leather and thudding hooves, and a neigh or a snort now and then. Surely the men expected Chance to do something, say something. But they also understood his reluctance. Norton's dreaded short fuse aside, when you are black and he is white, it is just that much harder to question your commander.

He couldn't help asking himself why Colonels MacKenzie and Davidson hadn't left those damn Indians alone to bake, to starve, and to thirst out here by themselves. Every Plains trooper knew that extreme weather was an Indian's greatest inducement to return to the reservation. For that matter, he wondered, could the Comanche themselves have forgotten that hunger had contributed to their surrender three years ago?

It wasn't long before one of his recruits fainted from sunstroke. Private Jones.

After Jones' fellow troopers jumped from their saddles to aid him where he landed in a puff of dust, Chance hastened down the line on his mount to check the man's canteen. Rattling the hollow vessel in the air, turning it upside down and waving it around, he demonstrated his subordinate's negligence to the entire column. For how long had Private Jones been riding dry? How many others were secretly dry as well? Chance cast looks at the miserable faces beneath those blue caps. Sympathy went just so far, caution and implied criticism farther still in the interest of his men's lives.

The command could not be put into greater jeopardy by stopping long to care for the indisposed. After the doctor was unable to revive Jones with a whiff of straight alcohol-laced cloth, the men assembled one of the two mesh sleds in their possession. Soon the troop was on the move again with the semi-conscious, babbling Jones rocking this way and that as he was dragged behind his horse, a yellow kerchief shielding his eyes from the sun.

Water. Chance kept telling himself it was too early in the season for water to vanish everywhere—a less than subtle form of denial. In fact, the only thing the men could anticipate with confidence was the nightly cooling-off hour, still perilously distant. With his worries beginning to get the better of his resolve, he resumed his place at the head of the column, where Norton's rigid jaw ruled. In the commander's expressed opinion, muttered man to man, Chance had contributed to the men's plight by not acting sooner to restrain their liquor consumption back at the supply camp. The recruits were too inexperienced to have known better, but not Chance. He should've anticipated their thirst the following day and how it would affect the march.

Chance took the criticism. There was simply no denying he should have been stricter. But if he could be faulted for looking the other way before a scout, it was Norton who'd entrusted their lives to Chivatá's story. Contrary to the plan mapped out in advance, she was leading them not along the known water route, but straight into the sandhills where she expected to cross the breakouts' trail. Leading them? She had merely ridden ahead.

What if Scott Renald hadn't sent her after all? What if this was a plot to deceive and doom the troop? The proof would be found in Chivatá's disappearance. Where would that leave the men?

Chance scanned the nothing that was their surroundings. Barely a bush, a root, a patch of brittle grass. He exhaled thick air from his lungs only to replace it with the same. His mouth was so dry that the simple act of swallowing trail food was painful. His lathered mount was weakening. Surely, by now, Norton must be regretting he hadn't sent a trooper or a Tonk ahead with Chivatá. Another error of command. Should she not reappear by sundown, they simply must about-face before dawn and head straight back to where water, however grainy, awaited them at Cedar Lake. By the time they got there, all their canteens would be dry. Of that, Chance was sure.

Chapter Twenty

Just after dawn on what for 10th Troop would have been Day One, Endah, riding abreast of Renald, spotted something. *"Dort!"* he exclaimed, pointing.

Far in the distance, galloping over a landscape of warming purples and brightening shades of bister and cedar, was a lone rider. Following Endah's gesture, Scott Renald strained his eyes. "A scout rushing a report to Fort Concho, I'd say." He regarded his uncomprehending companion. "But what am I wasting words on you for?"

He fired a shot in the air. The report seemed to carry to the ends of the earth, and it could've originated anywhere. Waving vigorously, Renald hoped to reveal their location on the desolate expanse. At first the speck merely slowed, but seconds later it was on the move again, making a beeline for them, and in a few minutes Trooper Tyler came bounding over a rise and pulled rein before the two mounted men with mules in tow.

"Mr. Renald!" he said with real excitement.

Smiling with familiarity, Renald replaced the spent bullet in the cylinder and snapped it shut with a practiced flick of the wrist. "Scott to you," he replied warmly. The scout's lathered charger appeared overworked, but Tyler surely knew the limits of his animal.

Tyler smiled. "Real good to see you, sir." In a single movement, he lowered his hand from his two-fingered salute to point at Endah. "And that must be Karl Hermann. Fit for a photograph."

Inexpressive on his pony, the brave merely held the scout's gaze.

"Nice hair," Tyler observed. "We heard you got him."

Renald was puzzled. How could they know at the supply base? Ben Ficklin's O'Bannon must have informed Colonel Davidson by wire. This suggested that Sergeant Chance had reached Ox Creek, a fact now confirmed by the trooper, who added, "… Talking Moon too. He arrived on a pass last night."

Tyler regarded their mules, laden with canteens and powder cans. "I see you's packing water. Much obliged for that—creek's on the sandy side, all but a trickle."

"I figured. Still, we're only packing a day's rations at best."

"That's gallons more than clang-empty."

"Unfortunately, Schmidt didn't have a galloper to send advance word. Has the troop—"

"Yessir, night march."

"Damn." Then Renald went on, "Why don't you walk with us a ways, Sergeant? Our horses could all use the rest." Without waiting for an answer, Renald dismounted. Endah, observing everything closely, slipped down as well. Tyler followed.

Renald inquired about the sergeant's mission back to Fort Concho.

"Your messenger got the intelligence to us just in time," replied Tyler.

Stunned, Renald responded, "What intelligence? And what messenger?"

"A fine looking one at that. She reported the breakouts' intent to join Caballero and Geronimo in New Mexico."

At first Renald's incredulous eyes sought out Endah. He wondered how much the brave understood. Possibly little besides the familiar names. Drawing his hand north instructively, he told the boy, "Chivatá—there—*mit army!*"

"More like, *there!*" Tyler thrust his gloved finger northwest. "From this point on the map, maybe two day's ride catch-up already."

Brow furled, the warrior revealed equal astonishment. "Chivatá?"

"She's heading the troop to a way-out place called Lost Lake," said Tyler. "Search me where it is. Somewhere beyond the caprock."

"The caprock? That's Fort Stanton's domain."

Tyler cocked his head. "We understood *you* was the source of the information, sir."

"Me?"

The three started on Tyler's trail north, with Tyler and his horse in the middle. Renald was trying to make sense of it all, chin down as his eyes searched the ground, then chin up as he searched the western skies. An attack on Fort Stanton? "I was aware of her intention to join the Apaches across the border," he replied, "but I certainly didn't send her, and I know nothing about a plan for the groups to unite."

"If she meant to join up with Caballero," said Tyler, "why on earth would she seek us out, pretending you sent her?"

"I'm as confounded as you are, Sergeant." But thinking back, Renald began to unravel the mystery. To Chivatá, he had revealed that Captain Norton, once charged with cowardice, was overeager to prove himself. Small talk at the time, this disclosure now amounted to a consequential misstep—a real blunder, he realized. Later, O'Bannon's voice had carried the Ox Creek news across the river while Chivatá was still present. From those pieces of information, Chivatá had formed her plot, whatever it might be in the end. After some setbacks of late, she was living up to her legend as smart, resourceful, and dangerous. Still struggling to grasp it all, Renald quickened his pace. "What about Talking Moon? Where's he in all this?"

Responding over the increased canteen-rattle and accelerated hoof-falls, Tyler continued, "MacKenzie sent him down from Fort Sill for influence. He's a real sight, that injun!"

"How do you mean?"

"For one thing, he's got blue eyes."

"Those are my sister's eyes, Sergeant."

Tyler peered into Renald's own pair of blue eyes with a look of discovery. "You done got 'em, too, ain'tcha! Well, that injun even dresses like a proper white man—store-bought suit, top hat. All business!"

Unfazed, Renald said, "He's all business, all right. He sells his longhorns to Cole Hawker. That same beef makes it back to the reservation as army handouts. If he's out here at the army's behest, it's for his own profit. What transpired when he arrived at the depot?"

"Chivatá translated for him."

Renald halted. A minute ago, he'd been worried; now he was gravely concerned. "*Translated,* did you say?"

Tyler stopped a stride ahead of him, then Endah a stride ahead of Tyler. "Yessir," said Tyler.

"But—Sergeant—their common language is *English*!"

Now it was Tyler's turn to express surprise. "I ain't heard no English coming from him!"

"Were you with them the whole time?"

The trooper shook his head. "At first it was just them two at the perimeter, plus the braves he was riding with."

"English didn't skip a generation in my family," said Renald, tension rising in his voice. "My sister—*his mother*—was a schoolteacher. What happened next?"

Tyler told him, and at last Renald divined the ruse. "That would suit Norton, wouldn't it? He gets the glory while Talking Moon merely gets the children—or so he was thinking."

Trooper Tyler beamed. "You done read the captain like a book!"

"So did the Indians, I'm afraid. Norton's been misinformed, misled."

Despite his obvious concern, Trooper Tyler kept his composure. His job was to act on and report intelligence, that was all. "Misled, sir?"

"According to Karl here, there's a Quahada camp much closer in." He asked Tyler if he had a survey map with him. When the trooper nodded, Renald flapped his fingers with urgency. "Let's have it."

The trooper dug into a saddle bag and retrieved a trail-worn, oily map of western Texas. With Endah looking over his shoulder, Renald unfolded it across his saddle. After a summary consultation, he pointed to a dot on the map. "*Here.* Just half a day's ride northeast of your depot."

"Rich Lake?" Tyler paled, a touch of trepidation in his voice. "If them renegades is there instead, that's real bad."

"They might not be there, but it's where Karl first learned about the breakout." *And Talking Moon would ensure its success,* he thought. "I can only guess what deal those two struck," he said, "after Chivatá ensured the command would look for Indians where there aren't any. My nephew will get his cut, I assure you."

Renald reverted to the map. He drew an imaginary line from the Ox Creek depot westward to Cedar Lake and then to Farther Lake beyond it. "Talking Moon's trajectory," he said, "according to traditional logic—following behind the breakouts and their plunder."

"That's where Davidson thought we should look," said Tyler. "He advised Captain Norton to start by scouting lake to lake."

"You know the Comanche as well as I do, trooper. And I say this looks too easy. Where do *they* think we'll look for them? And now Norton, who massacred the Northern People, is being led over the caprock by an Apache? *Not good.*"

Renald met Tyler's alarmed eyes before returning to the map. "We're about here …" He traced a line with his finger to Cedar Lake and then swept it far to the northwest—past the white dunes, past even the escarpment caprock. "Lost Lake," he announced, "somewhere in there." He righted himself. "Karl says Cedar Lake is dry. That's bad enough. But if Lost Lake is dry too—they're dead."

"Shit," said Tyler. "Even if there *is* water, Chivatá wins. The breakouts get through—only by another route."

Renald hung his head in exasperation. Finally, he looked up. "I'll ride this relief up to Cedar Lake and see if I can't pick up Norton's trail."

"I oughta switch with you, sir. I'm sure to find it. And you can inform of the troop movement instead."

"You're duty bound, trooper—and now you've got even more to report to Command. I'll see you back at the depot in a few days—if we're lucky." Now Renald addressed Endah. "The men that saved your brother—*here.*" He pounded the map with his finger, then purposefully grasped a fistful of his horse's mane. "Black men."

Endah simply blinked. Did he understand?

"Chivatá take them there," said Renald, speaking as plainly as he could. "They will die. *Ellos morirán.* You can save them."

The brave's face flushed. His cheeks seemed to rise and withdraw while his lips cracked open.

"I don't get it, sir," Tyler remarked. "And I suspect he don't, neither. You letting him go?"

"Question is what he makes of it," Renald answered. He grasped Endah's shoulder. "*Frei.* You're *frei!*"

Endah's eyes widened—but with the realization of what sort of opportunity? Merely to go *frei,* or to do something with that freedom? And for whom, Renald wondered. Without a word of parting—indeed, like a wild thing unchained—the white warrior vaulted onto his horse and took off north over stone and sand, kicking up maroon dust. His hoofbeats drummed across the prairie.

Nodding after him, Renald observed, "He saved me at least once yesterday. Now he could do the same for your men."

But Tyler knew how the desert got a man thinking. "Who's to say how his thoughts'll turn out there," he pondered.

Renald saluted. "Good luck, Sergeant."

Returning the gesture, Tyler answered, "To us all, Scott." With that, he swung up onto his animal and hauled her around, then bounded off toward Fort Concho on a simmering landscape now painted in ochre and siennas.

Chapter Twenty-one

At dusk on Day Three the men were pitching camp in the sandhills without protest from Sergeant Chance, despite his reservations. Everybody knew that questioning Norton's orders always ended badly. Thus, when his commander decided to bivouac the troop, Tops yet again elected to hold his tongue. Nevertheless, he couldn't restrain regrets about his earlier acquiescence. His experience told him they should have accompanied Talking Moon to Farther Lake, thereby trusting neither Indian, rather than both. At Farther Lake they might have found the women and children and deduced that the braves were still out here, somewhere. Or they might have found the Indians undivided—or found none at all. But rather than checking all these possibilities, they were simply churning up the pale desert sand in utter ignorance, frustration, and growing panic.

Despite hopes to the contrary, what if the breakouts were *east* of them?—at Rich Lake or Mound Lake or Tahoka Lake? Might these lakes be less parched? They didn't know, but Chance guessed the hostiles did. In any case, at this stage nobody but their commander was principally concerned about finding Indians. As for Chivatá, to the surprise of those like Chance who had suspected her, she returned before dark. Calls arose announcing her arrival at the northern perimeter, prompting Chance to drive a final stake into the ground signaling a newly erected tent before he stepped away to escort her into Norton's presence.

Chance dragged himself through camp with his tongue clicking dry in his mouth, his gums aching. The men were all suffering the same or worse. Even in favorable climate conditions, a half-gallon canteen could only last a trooper about twenty-four hours if emptied responsibly. Having shared some grainy water with a needier subordinate and lost more to his mount, Chance's canteen was already about empty. Soon, he knew, the horses would start dropping, and the men would have to resort to drinking their blood. Troopers who'd completely drained their canteens by now were filling them with their own urine, afraid to just piss it away. While Norton had condoned this practice and broken out the sugar to make it more palatable, the army doc cautioned the cycle ought not be repeated. Second and third rounds would dry the body further and cause even more thirst, he said.

Reporting to Norton in his sparsely furnished tent, Chivatá was afforded a folding stool opposite him while the doc had a look at her wound. Chance, for his part, stood by the door flap with locked hands, attentive. The slightest of breezes pressed against the canvas behind her.

"The trail was made on firm ground," she said, "six or seven miles northwest of here."

The doc raised the back of her shirt.

She forced the front side down in her grasp, continuing. "Perhaps forty mounts heading toward the caprock." To

Chance, it sounded too good to be true—that they might find everything they were looking for in one place.

Removing the dressing, the bearded sawbones was satisfied by what he saw. "The inflammation is reduced in amount and color, and a scab has formed with no liquid material present," he told Norton over the patient's shoulder. Then, releasing the back of her shirt, he unburdened her of the arm sling. "No need … It's going to be sore, but you're out of danger. Doubtless the dry conditions have aided the healing."

Out of danger—an unfortunate turn of phrase considering the men's difficulties. Norton abruptly ordered the doctor out.

To Chance, observing, Chivatá appeared remarkably fresh— in fact, looking far from trail-dusty, she appeared *washed*. On top of that, her vitality had rebounded. He found himself wondering why the only wounded person among them was visibly more vital than everybody else.

"When you see the sign," she was saying, "you will know that I am telling the truth. Follow it, and we will find water. We will find Lost Lake."

But was this simply a ruse to lure the command even deeper into the desert?

Although Chivatá brought the news they'd been waiting for, Norton and Chance exchanged looks. If the sign was genuine and the hostiles eventually joined forces with Caballero across the border, the remote post of Fort Stanton and its sister troop would be threatened. Chance, again overriding his concern for his own men, accepted that Norton must confront this peril. Thus, he swallowed any protest when ordered by Norton to prepare the troop to march before sunrise.

* * *

Day Four began with the troop on the move in the drafty coolness of the wee hours. Despite their fatigue, much progress was made under the starry sky, and by the time the lavenders and blues of dawn began yielding to fiery hues, the men and their horses practically stumbled out of the dunes onto more fertile terrain. At last the white sands were behind them, but before long the sun would be beating down on their suffering selves, drawing the day's first beads of sweat. Able to graze now, the horses seemed better off than the men, and they smelled better too.

With the blanket of darkness lifted, they saw the escarpment for the first time as an infinite, rusted blur on the horizon atop the prairie's wash of yellows and dotted grayish greens. A rugged, two-hundred-mile-long sandstone curvature, it zigzagged northeast before veering west, rising a thousand feet at its highest.

Not far from the caprock's base, their path crossed the tracks previously reported by Chivatá. Rediscovering them, she sat triumphantly on her pony as hot gusts whipped her shoulder-length hair, uneven from her ritual mourning sacrifice. She drew a line with her finger due west toward the vast and towering caprock, about five miles distant.

Norton was first to slide from his saddle, somewhat unsteadily—or so thought Chance. The commander bent down on one knee for a closer look at the sign. To him it seemed made by just seven or eight riders: "… and it's hardly fresh," he complained.

Chivatá argued that the dry conditions affected its perceived age, and the band's tight, drawn-out riding formation had allowed them to cloak their true numbers. To Chance, while what she said was commonly true of Indian tactics, her reliability was increasingly doubtful. And yet, given their ever more trying circumstances, they couldn't afford to dismiss her conclusions outright. He dismounted to get a closer look while Norton maintained his own doubting interest in this unusual, solitary trail—as if mulling the purchase of potential snake oil.

After a cursory glance at the tracks, Chance observed, "They're supposed to be riding with a lotta plunder—shod horses and longhorn. I ain't seeing none of that."

She was firm. "I told you, the livestock stays with the women and children while the men join others to attack Fort Stanton. Do you doubt that an Indian woman can look after livestock or ride like a man?"

Incredulous, Norton shook his head. He rose with effort. "Maybe you heard wrong."

She struck a haughty tone. "It is your choice. These Indians are headed over the caprock toward Lost Lake. Follow them or not."

"But we ain't got a map extends that far west!" The words were uttered by Corporal Miller, who'd just ridden up the line, reviewing its sorry condition. "Meantime, the men's losing their minds."

Chance inhaled scorching air. "And we can't rely on water between them dunes we just left and them to the north. Closest seasonal lake is a day's ride in that direction, by my reckoning."

A fretting brow revealed Norton's distress at driving the troop further west with only this meager sign to go on. He told Chivatá, "Indian trail often peters out. That happens, we'll have to rely on *you* to find water."

Chivatá sat motionless, expressionless. Then, "I need to drink too."

"Do you?" Norton asked.

Chance cut in, his tone merely informational. "Fort Stanton's about ninety miles due west."

Crossing his arms over his chest—bracing himself—Norton conceded, "I'd sure feel better if Trooper Tyler was with us."

Chance could not know that Norton's West Point education was haunting him. Had not Marcus Licinius Crassus at the head of his legions been led astray and to his death by a swarthy desert guide?

Chance traced his mustache with his thumb and forefinger—a sign of reflection. "But you done right running our most reliable scout south with that intelligence," he responded, finally. "Don't doubt that, sir."

Norton bowed his head. "I was right at the time. We've got too many days behind us now ..." His voice, like his gaze, trailed off.

"Not if we can refill our canteens at Cedar Lake." This time Chance put his own men first, despite the possible threat to Fort Stanton and its fellow black troop. Fact was, Chance and his men were in no shape to chase Indians, let alone fight them. Just mounting up was a painful affair, and some of his men were having to be tied to their saddles. "We can still make it back. Hope goes a long way."

Norton shook his head again. "We gotta make Lost Lake. If Fort Stanton's in trouble ..."

"*If*, sir."

This unhinged Norton. His dreaded temper exploded like a geyser. "You're testing my limits, Tops! *Don't.*"

With that, Norton groaned up onto his horse, heedless of his spent men.

"But, sir—respectfully—how come we don't request volunteers for a water detail to Cedar Lake? Divide the risk."

Norton gripped his saddle horn, agonizing. Clearly he feared he would be sending men to their deaths in the sandhills. Men he needed, respected. At last, he invited Corporal Miller to comment on the condition of the troop.

Miller roused his mount forward. He was a younger man whose face, usually clean shaven, was bristling with patches of growth. After a pained look, he reported, "Following Private Jones' passing yesterday, among the weakest is privates Roberts, Isaacs, and Rose. Corporal Barney's tongue is hanging from his mouth like a stone-dry sponge."

"And Corporal Devans?" Norton tapped his temple. "I didn't like where he was going earlier."

"Devans is in bad shape too. Besides that, Private Wilson's horse just died. He's presently mounted on Trooper Jones' horse. We'll lose more horses today, putting soldiers on foot. There's no mount strong enough anymore to seat two men."

As if it were any consolation, Norton responded, "With conditions this bad, those breakouts must be suffering mightily as well. I'll bet life at Fort Sill is looking *real* comfy right now."

"Captain," added Chance in his gravest tone yet, "what if you're right? Maybe they got more than they bargained for too."

The actual situation as described by Miller, followed by the hypothetical one proposed by Chance, combined to affect Norton. Tears were a selfish luxury during a thirst, and as if to hide glassy eyes, he blinked up at the sky. "If we don't find water soon," he confessed, "the command is lost!"

Though his statement was unfitting to his rank, at least Norton had finally acknowledged the full gravity of the crisis. Even to him it was now about finding water—not Indians.

Norton pinched his eyes shut. He gathered himself, and met Chance's sympathetic gaze. "Tops, you have my orders to select and dispatch four men to Cedar Lake for the purposes of replenishing the troop's water supply. Should they not find water, they will proceed with godspeed to the supply point."

"Yessir!"

"Take volunteers willing to drink their own, or their horses'—while it lasts," Norton added. "Only the hero-type will make the difference."

Despite this momentous turn, Chance saluted with somewhat less than his usual vigor. "Yes, sir—thank you, sir."

Chapter Twenty-two

In the afternoon of Day Three, Renald stopped at Cedar Lake—not quite as dry as Karl had reported, but dry indeed it was to the eye.

Before long, he found signs that 10th Troop had already been there and dug successfully for water. He patiently refilled the two canteens he had consumed en route and watered his animals. He also found fresh, shod tracks leading westward on the known route to Farther Lake, made by a small party, presumably Talking Moon's on his army-issue mounts. By contrast, the troop's distinctive sign diverted northwest from here toward the sandhills. Besides being wider and messier, these included horse and pack mule tracks, and—unsurprisingly by this point—a pair of lines three feet apart, doubtless made by a stretcher. The column couldn't be moving very fast, but his own speed was necessarily hampered by his laden mules.

Toward dusk, with the dunes appearing like a dark, ruffled blanket in the distance, he noticed a freshly dug grave off to the side. That it was marked by a mere strung-together mesquite cross suggested the men were traveling so lean they had nothing to spare for one. The name *Jones* was scratched on the mound.

Renald, who knew the Llano's secrets as well as any white man, made his way northwest through familiar arroyos and stony passes in the sandstone ribbing. He was gaining on the troop, but if Norton kept pressing ahead, no options remained to overtake him except a night ride. With little wind to speak of, the command's tracks proved easy to follow by the moon and starlight, even after he'd entered the dunes. In the small hours he let the animals blow while he stayed awake, careful not to fall into a slumber whose duration could last till sunrise. About noon the next day he reached the edge of the dunes, witnessing the prairie open up beneath the never-ending arc of the caprock. He had made it here with all his animals, and judging by the path he was on, so had the men at least this far and a bit farther still. Their fate could be determined by the health and maintenance of his animals. He decided to rest again.

After stripping down the mules, he let them and his horse graze on the plentiful switchgrass and bluestem—a real treat after the slim pickings offered by the sandhills. As for himself, he took the opportunity to luxuriate with a pot of coffee. In no time he'd started a small fire and was boiling a modest portion for himself, aware that every drop was precious. Having forgone sleep, his head was pounding. The kettle soon began to rattle. As he reached for it with a gloved hand, something drew his attention to a nearby patch of juniper. A line of mounted men began to emerge from behind it—black cavalrymen in dark blue uniforms coated with powder. In tow were four mules laden with canteens like his—and yet not like his: Renald could hear their hollow clanking.

Eying the camp, the lead rider spurred his sluggish, dusty charger forward and came to a lumbering halt above Renald. It was a barely recognizable Corporal Miller. Recognizing Renald, he practically gasped his name.

Renald could hear sand in the soldier's throat. His skin tone was a kind of grey, his eyes yellowed. His exclamation surely cost him dear energy.

Holding the kettle in one hand and his tin cup in the other, Renald rose on stiff knees. He motioned with his sloshing cup toward the stack of canteens and powder cans. "At your service, Corporal …"

"Them full?" Miller asked, thirst in his voice.

"It's no mirage!" Renald answered. "Courtesy of Lieutenant Schmidt at Fort Concho."

But Schmidt couldn't solely be credited for this remarkable turn of fortune, and Miller gave Renald a grand, skin-splitting smile, probably his first in days. "From afar we been confounded by them glints! Mind if we help usselves?"

Given his notoriety as a former Confederate officer, Scott Renald was hardly popular with the soldiers of the 10th, but at this moment he seemed to have no history. He liked that. "Go easy at the start," he cautioned them all. "Just wet your whistles."

Their eerily leaden faces lit up as the men came stumbling from their saddles. Out front in their rush for refreshment was Miller himself, his excited smile constant. Reaching the shiny heap first, he hauled up a canteen to demonstrate its weight for the others. Then, forgoing a first swig, he lobbed it at one of his subordinates. The young trooper—skinny as a scarecrow—accepted it with a tantalizing thud in his embrace. It nearly knocked him over. Disregarding Renald's advice, the private hefted it above his head and took a face-splattering guzzle before passing it on.

Watching the men excitedly pass the vessel around—chasing their swallows with gulps of air as if surfacing from underwater—Renald realized he had instantly rehabilitated himself with the troop. "It ain't much," he added, "but it's sufficient to get your men well on their way back."

"*It ain't much?*" a soldier exclaimed between sloppy pulls. "Johnny Reb done saved us!"

"Got food tins and hardtack," Renald offered.

"Oh, we got plenty o' food rations," Miller responded. "Damned if we been able to get anything down our dry gullets." Accepting the canteen for a second round, he asked, "There's yet some water at Cedar Lake?"

Renald confirmed it, and indicated the caprock. "None ahead, I take it."

"Not a drop," Miller confessed, his wetted voice fuller. He passed the canteen to his subordinate. "Private Avery, water the animals with the remainder."

Gesturing toward the canteens, Renald said, "See those two off to the side there? They were refilled at Cedar Lake. You can use 'em for the animals."

"You done thought this through," said Miller. He folded his legs, indicating to his men that they should rest too.

Renald sat himself down as the soldiers stretched their legs. He filled his cup from the kettle. "Coffee's not recommended following your ordeal," he said, "but help yourselves."

Beaming, Miller extended his open hand, and Renald—after a moment's awkward hesitation—shared his cup with him. He inquired about the troop's position.

Miller gulped his coffee down, then said, "Climbing the caprock by now, I expect." He smacked his lips at the bitter delight and passed the cup behind to the others. "Them's following a trail to someplace called Lost Lake," Miller continued.

Renald simply replied, "Folly …"

"Sir?"

"Is Chivatá still with you?"

"Last I knew …"

"Whatever she might've told Norton," said Renald, "I didn't send her. But I did send somebody else to warn you about her, somebody who might've helped you find water."

"Ain't nobody joined the command but her," said Miller.

Renald found himself focusing on a prickly shrub to Miller's side. What else could he tell Trude Hermann than that he'd had Karl, but let him go. It was as it should be. Endah could not be extracted from this environment and made a house pet—not anymore.

Still, when the boy rode north yesterday, just where had he gone?

Miller extended the cup, now empty, in his hand. Rather than receiving it, Renald emptied the kettle into it and Miller passed it back to his men.

"Trooper Tyler told me how Chivatá presented herself to Norton," said Renald. He cleared his throat, squinting. "I don't suppose Norton's noticed that just about every Indian in this story is unaccounted for, while every one of *us* is wandering around in a heat wave. That's no coincidence."

"The captain is stubborn as a mule—respectfully speaking, of course. But Chivatá needs water, too, so we's sticking with her."

Feeling Norton's predicament, Renald shook his head. "And Tops Chance?"

"He's doing his best, but we's beginning to fail. Some men's strapped to their saddles, some's having trouble seeing, even hearing. A few's got tongues so swollen their mouths can't shut. Horses ain't much better off, as you can see."

Renald nodded gravely. "I stopped at Trooper Jones' grave back there, but Sergeant Chance will see you through."

"You say Chance, but not Norton?" Miller handed Renald the coffee cup, empty again.

"I owe my own life to Emanuel Chance." His gaze intensified. "You still got Tonk scouts with you?"

"Them's plumb useless, not knowing the area, but so loyal they ain't run off."

Renald had inquired for a different reason. "I best turn back," he concluded. With the water detail accomplished, he needn't risk coming in contact with tribesmen whose chief he'd killed in Laura Little's rescue. "I'll ride to the depot to ensure water and supplies are brought forward to Cedar Lake."

With that, he strained to his feet. Miller followed him up and helped collect his things. Finally, the corporal kicked dust over the smoldering kindling. Renald climbed onto his mount, and the grateful men exchanged vigorous salutes with him.

They wished each other luck, with Miller adding, "And bless you for the water."

Renald swung eastward and quickly disappeared over a ragged eminence.

Chapter Twenty-three

Lost Lake was a playa lake merely a hundred feet in diameter, bordered on its far side by a scattering of mesquite trees. While not deep, being situated on the high Llano and at the bottom of a gradual depression, it tended to go dry later in the season than other lakes. It attracted buffalo and Indians alike, though few of either were left in these parts to partake.

For everybody but Captain Norton the sole purpose of today's scout was to survive long enough to reach the supply point. That meant finding refreshment. In the hours leading up to now, there was no denying that the drought, combined with their commander's relentless ambition, posed an existential threat to the troop. But his ambition aside, so too would a retreat to Cedar Lake have endangered the men. This was the dilemma that afflicted every man's thoughts. This was why nobody had yet confronted Norton—really confronted him. The price of dissent, of disrupting the troop's cohesion, could not be reasonably calculated against the obedience that had gotten them this far. On their ascent of the escarpment alone, two horses had collapsed without a trace of froth issuing from their mouths. Putting them down had left three men on foot, in shifts, further slowing the troop. Private Jones had died yesterday, and with his expiration auguring the worst—and a ranting, feverish Corporal Devans seemingly near his own end—morale in the ranks had sunk to a new low. In hours, if not minutes, more troopers would fall—and more horses as well. Before long, a sizable portion of the command would be on foot.

Approaching the lake from behind a grassy rise to its east, the men began to fear the worst about their destination when, after days of whiffing nothing at all in the blazing heat, a gut-wrenching stench enveloped them. It was accompanied—inauspiciously—by an endless swarm of deer flies the size of marbles, which thudded against cheeks hollowed by dehydration and buzzed by ears accustomed to desert silence. Even before the head of the column reached the hilltop, every able-minded soldier had covered his nose and mouth with his neckerchief. Norton and Chance were no exceptions.

Reaching the crest, Chance responded to his commander's muffled order to halt by signaling the column with a raised hand.

"Cruel fate," Norton remarked about the scene before them, referring either to what he saw or its impact on his men. He clasped his saddle horn with both gloved hands, as if clinging to it. "Never in all my years ..." he muttered.

With the afternoon sun blasting their faces full on, the troopers at the front of the line shared a speechless horror. Dozens of bloated carcasses—bison, pronghorn, and coyote— all caked with mud and crawling with flies, lay on the cracked, hardening lake bottom—a buffalo wallow turned beast trap. Thirst had brought these animals here, but not even the men's hung-necked horses sniffed water worth drinking. Their ears flattened in despair. Meantime, scores of quail and snipes playfully dust-bathed around the lake's perimeter, as if in mockery of the men and their animals.

Norton slumped in his saddle with an aggrieved sigh. What now? Everybody was suffering a starvation of hope equal to his thirst. How much more could they endure? How much longer could they go on? By this point, most of their canteens were sloshing with either urine or horse blood, and those who hadn't resorted to such extremes found that not even sugar would dissolve in their mouths. Their bodies had stopped producing saliva as well as the tears they might have shed.

In the stench and onslaught of flies, the half-mad Corporal Devans abandoned his horse with a howling cry and staggered toward the muddy swath, arms flailing against the sun's glare. He collapsed onto all fours like some desperate beast and sank his nose in a pool of tainted, alkaline muck. Two men managed to yank him out quickly, but he would expire the next day.

The commander turned his glare on Chivatá. She was saddled to his left, a bandanna concealing her expression. "Well, what now?" he snapped.

Through the cloth over her lips, she replied, "I will scout another waterhole."

Hearing this, Norton tore the scarf from his own face, exposing his dusty beard. "*Scout?* Run off, more like—now that you've achieved your aim. I'll horsewhip you for this!"

Chin up, she responded simply. "I do not fear you, *Capitán.*"

"You don't defend yourself either," he fired back.

Damn her, thought Chance, smoothing his mustache behind the scarf. But, for him, it was time to confront Norton, not Chivatá. His commander was clenching his reins with threatening intensity and Chance feared he would truly lash her with them. He should beware her weapon: following the doctor's clean bill of health, she'd received her gun back. Chance kept his hand near his own sidearm.

"Captain Norton," he said, "the troop can rest in that timber yonder, while we scout for water."

Norton's response was biting. "*Obviously*, Sergeant. But if a new water detail yields nothing, it means ending yet another scout without engaging the enemy, and returning with a *shocking* loss of life and livestock!" He gasped for breath before turning on Chivatá:

"If there's other lakes out here, then why all this *Lost Lake*!— *Lost Lake*!—*Lost Lake*!" He thrust his finger at her. "At best you intended to lead us astray, at worst to our doom! Is that why you haven't vanished already—because you enjoy seeing us drop dead one by one?"

The whole troop was witness to this outburst, and it made Chance cringe. He glanced back at the men, most of their expressions obscured by their cavalry yellow neckerchiefs. Norton's temper—triggered—was what he and all the others feared and why no serious protest had been made till now.

"It is not my fault we have not found water," she answered, unconvincingly.

"Haven't you? We'll see about that!"

Spurring his horse against her pony, Norton leaned over and ripped away her canteen. Dust from the hoof-scuffle powdered the air. She reined her mount back, putting distance between them. For all to see, he heaved the canteen in the billowing haze, announcing, "Heavy with water!"

Then, swinging it to the nearest trooper, he called down the line, "Go on! Pass it back, have a swig each! On her!"

The formation was already loosening with thirsty anticipation.

On the receiving end of the canteen-toss, the trooper tugged down his scarf. His first attempt to drink resulted in a fit of gagging. Then, after resisting another soldier's grab at the vessel, he got some down with difficulty.

Norton reined again toward Chivatá. "Others," he spat, "were surprised when you returned from scouting the dunes. They thought you'd surely made off. But what struck me—and Sergeant Chance here too—was how *fresh* you looked when you came back. Like a watered prairie flower! You led us straight past their camp, didn't you? And not a dry camp!"

That she did not react was telling.

"You struck a deal with Talking Moon, eh? To lead the troop into nowhere while he rounds up the renegades himself?"

Chance wondered if Norton wasn't too far off. Behind them were the sandhills. If Chivatá wasn't a hapless scout, it was a fair deduction that she was cooperating with a disloyal Talking Moon to—finally—deliver a bounty to Geronimo or Caballero here in New Mexico. After all, back at the supply point she had made a beeline for the Comanche emissary and exchanged words with him before anybody else could. But even if this were the case, and she had knowingly led them astray to give Talking Moon a head start, several failures of command had led them to this point, and neither he nor Captain Norton could deny that inwardly.

Outwardly was another matter. Chance was already preparing his own explanations for the inquest that would certainly follow.

Yet resorting to explanations was only the survivor's privilege. First, they had to make it back. It was an opportune moment to sway their commander—for if Norton had finally acknowledged Chivatá's duplicity, then he too had become convinced they were tracking ghosts.

But it was too late for talk.

Norton reached for his service revolver.

"Captain Norton, sir!"

A tight look of preparedness in her eyes, Chivatá reined her pony back a step. "Don't do it," she warned.

Undeterred, Norton drove his charger forward, ramming her pony's side. Half a foot closer and he would have crushed her leg.

This was an extraordinary action. Chance recognized that a loss of control at the top would cause instant, deleterious effects on the men. Pulling his neckerchief from his face, he spurred after the feuding pair, feeling like he was following them over a cliff as his men looked on. Murmurs arose from the column, its cohesion cracking. Never more than now, the troop needed decisive leadership.

"Captain!" he cried again, coming alongside Norton as his commander drove Chivatá further back with the pressure of his butting charger and pointed gun.

Though her first instinct must have been to draw on Norton, the woman warrior acted with curious restraint. Instead, she pulled the cloth from her mouth as if to speak—to protest? To confess? To declare victory? But before she could say anything, Chance managed to wedge his mount between the two parties and shield her.

"Not like this," he entreated. "Not in front of the men …"

Rage reddened Norton's face. "You! Taking this perfidious squaw's side?"

Chance again reminded himself that Norton had recently lost his wife, that he was a suffering, grieving man. But in taking this into consideration, he paused too long.

"Intent on losing those stripes, Sergeant?" Norton bellowed.

"Sir—think this through! It's ..."

But words again failed Chance. With his heart pounding, a general weakness overcame him. He couldn't—as Norton had put it—take her side. Exerting his steadfast loyalty to the U.S. Cavalry, he shifted his horse back into alignment with his commander.

Crack! An arrow pierced Norton's chest—and a bulge appeared in the back of his topcoat.

Norton's eyes flashed with the injustice of the thing. He teetered sideways.

Heedless of the danger, Chance and others alighted from their saddles, hastening to catch their commander on his way down. Chance was first to struggle with the big man's dead weight, and as he did so, he called for the entire troop to dismount. "Use your horses for cover!" he cried. Suddenly, in this parched place, came coursing fluid in the form of Norton's warm blood spilling through Chance's fingers and soaking his cuffs and sleeves. He attempted to lay Norton down, but the arrow though the commander's back propped him up. Eyes and mouth agape, Norton's head rolled to one side. With troopers easing the man's body down onto one shoulder, Chance pivoted around on one knee toward where Chivatá had been standing.

Gone.

As her absence registered, he heard the hoofbeats. He got on his feet and spotted her silhouette hightailing it away. From the side another drum of hoofbeats now arose, and he became aware of a shadowy flash between the trees across the dry lake: Norton's attacker, escaping. Jaw lined with tension, Chance unloaded his weapon into the trees. Others around him joined in the shooting, their reports thunderous across the escarpment. Little birds fluttered into flight en masse and some went down in the shooting frenzy. Finally, Chance heard himself yelling for his men to stop—the last order he would give as second-in-command. He glared across the expanse. Chivatá had made her escape northwest—first, past the fly-infested carcasses, then over the bosky rise across the lake.

Emanuel Chance would not call on his broken men to perform the impossible and lay pursuit. With the threat gone as quickly as it had come, his first duty was to his wounded senior officer. Turning back and holstering his gun, he saw two soldiers kneeling at Captain Norton's side, bracing his mass, while the surgeon worked a wide cutter from behind.

A grisly snap split the air, and the sawbones pulled back with the tool. One of the supporting troopers raised himself, gripping a segment of the shaft, its arrowhead smeared with blood and dirt. The other men laid Norton flat on his back.

The doc flashed his hopelessness to Chance as the sergeant approached. Below them, the Irishman lay still in an expanding pool of blood, a death-glare in his unblinking blue eyes, his mouth agape, his black beard powdered with the stuff of his final scout. Chance kneeled and gently shuttered Norton's eyes.

Then, exchanging remorseful looks with the men, he scrutinized the shaft embedded in the chest of his late commander. "Ever seen anything like it? An arrow that long?"

"Never," came somebody's reply.

"That's Apache fletching if I ever seen it," offered somebody else.

"The feathers might be Apache," said Chance, "but the arrow's length ain't." He planted his palms on his thighs and rose.

His men, satisfied the threat had passed, drifted out from behind their animals for a glimpse of their fallen commander and to pay their respects. Just minutes after Norton had threatened to demote him, Sergeant Chance got to his feet as their senior officer in charge, the man who would get most of them home.

Chapter Twenty-four

Renald was finishing lunch on the patio when Luís, in his white blouse, rounded the corner with a uniformed galloper, lightly dusted from the trail. Patting the corners of his mouth with his napkin, Renald rose to his feet to greet this army messenger. The corporal promptly saluted and presented him with an envelope bearing the seal of Fort Mc-Kavett. It came as no surprise to Renald—but so soon as his very first day back?

"Urgent summons, sir."

"Meaning I return with you?" Renald grumbled.

"That's the idea."

With legs still stiff from the journey home and a bad hip joint smarting, Renald dreaded the distance he must ride to the regimental inquest—and before he could see Trude Hermann again. He'd been thinking a lot about what he was going to say to her.

Sighing, he gave Luís a nod, and his foreman told the soldier, "You are invited to dine." With a wink, he added, "My wife cooks good."

The young man brightened. "Thanking you kindly," he replied, removing his cap. "I sure could eat."

To the right of Renald's plate at the head of the table, Luís pulled a chair, and the corporal and his host took their seats. Renald didn't bother to initiate conversation, leaving the soldier to break the awkward silence. "I see you're catching up on your reading, sir …"

Renald glanced disappointedly at the newspaper lying beside his coffee cup. Plain to see was its callous headline: *Norton's Lost Nigger Expedition.* He shook his head. Those brave troopers deserved better than this, their late commander worse.

Luís poured their caller a cup of coffee, and Renald met the youth's unbothered gaze. "My testimony will be clear," he said. "It was *Norton's* lost expedition—simple as that."

* * *

In all, four soldiers and their commander were dead. What went wrong? The hearing, ordered by Department commander Brigadier General Edward Ord to explore the circumstances of the ill-fated scout, was conducted by Fort McKavett's commander, Major Thomas Anderson, and his First Lieutenant, E.O. Gibson. In accord with Renald's own assessment, it found the late Captain Norton "grossly negligent in his judgment," while commending the actions of Sergeants Chance and Tyler, as well as those of Lieutenant Schmidt and Corporal Miller— all of whom were present to give testimony. Renald, however, did not come out of it so well. For his decision to unleash Karl Hermann, thereby aborting his mission and indirectly causing Norton's death, he received a reprimand; merely that because, in Major Anderson's view, his initiative to run water to the lost command had, in fact, saved it. On its opinion page, the influential *Fort Worth Democrat* would interpret this judgment as "an official slap on the wrist, remedied by a casual clap on the shoulder."

For his part, Colonel MacKenzie, up at Fort Sill, was praised for dispatching Talking Moon to find the renegades and return them to the reservation.

Contrary to Renald's suspicions, the breakouts weren't at Rich Lake after all, or for that matter anywhere in the vicinity of Farther Lake. Instead, as Talking Moon had recounted to Colonel MacKenzie upon his return, after "exploring" the salt flats west of the bone-dry Farther Lake, he rode north to "discover" the warriors and their families sheltering by a spring in the dunes south of the caprock. To Renald, this seemed an illogical deviation on Talking Moon's part—unless the exploration of Farther Lake had indeed been a ruse to shake off Norton. The sandhills that yielded the breakouts were those through which both 10th Troop and Renald had passed on their fateful journeys toward Lost Lake.

By his nephew's account, as reported in court by Colonel MacKenzie's office, the breakout leader Teneverka was easily convinced to return to the reserve. Teneverka had not foreseen how unseasonably extreme weather and a privation of buffalo could combine to threaten all their lives. They could not safely venture far from the spring. According to the calendar, Teneverka and his followers set out for Fort Sill with antelope skins bulging with water the very day Norton lost his life at Lost Lake. At the same time, Renald was in transit from Cedar Lake to the supply camp at Ox Creek.

Renald believed his Comanche nephew's report up to a point. Neither Talking Moon nor Norton wanted to ride together and, more likely than not, Talking Moon knew where to look for Teneverka. Perhaps his nephew had even prearranged to meet the breakout chief in the sandhills to deal in the stolen horses, many of which were later reported to have expired in the desert.

As for Chivatá's scouting for 10th Troop, when Renald heard Chance's testimony about her full canteen and refreshed appearance at Lost Lake, he became convinced that she had stopped off at Teneverka's secret spring camp. To him, this was proof—not simply evidence—of a plot between her and Talking Moon to doom the troop.

Although Renald made his suspicions known to the panel, as far as the army brass were concerned, Talking Moon had successfully completed his mission, while the luckless Captain Norton had failed. That Indians couldn't be trusted was a given, argued Major Anderson, and distrust of them should have factored into success for Norton rather than failure. In the end, nobody would ever know the Indians' true intentions— for why should they?

* * *

Not until Renald and Mrs. Hermann finally met at Martha's Restaurant-Saloon did she learn of her eldest son's connection to the lost expedition. As she followed Renald's story—from his early encounter with Chivatá to Karl's reported murder of the medicine man, and later to Karl's capture and release— her slice of apple pie went untouched and her coffee grew cold. Renald spoke slowly and carefully to her, wanting to be sure she understood every word.

"With the water-run in *my* hands," he was telling her amidst lunch chatter and porcelain clinks, "I sent Karl ahead to warn the troop about Chivatá. I hoped he would recognize his debt to them for saving Freddie. Whether he'd been tracking the troop or was simply waiting for them at Lost Lake, I don't know."

Her head sank at the suggestion that her son had taken yet another white life—and an army captain's life at that. Perhaps she was thinking of Karl's father and his army service back in the old country. Had Captain Norton's coarseness recalled Gunter's? Was killing him a reaction to the memory of Gunter disciplining young Karl with the back of a hairbrush? But these were neither Mrs. Hermann's thoughts nor Renald's.

"In my view," Renald continued, "Endah can't be blamed for defending a member of his tribe. Why, even Sergeant Chance tried to stop Norton."

Trude Hermann leaned forward, her bosom—he noticed—resting on the laced cloth. "But how do you know Karl did it? The killer of Captain Norton, nobody saw."

"The arrow," he answered. "Sergeant Chance presented it at the inquest. No Indian packs a four-foot arrow—no Indian except Karl Hermann. As Chief Tall Grass put it, *Great is his bow.*" He squared his shoulders with conviction. "At Fort Concho there's a lieutenant named Schmidt who noticed that bow before we even set out. He thinks Karl fashioned it after the heroes of fable books. I reckon you know which ones."

Her brown eyes narrowed. "Oh, dear," she lamented.

"Refill, Mr. Renald?"

It was the aproned proprietress, Martha, practically jabbing him in the face with a kettle.

"Sure beats trail coffee," he replied jovially, craning his neck.

"Glad you got back in one piece."

"Wish I hadn't returned empty handed, though …"

"Empty handed?" Martha offered Trude a look of incredulity. "Mr. Renald, if you hadn't been out there for Mrs. Hermann, who knows what worse might've befallen that troop?" She poured his refill and withdrew, with an admiring—even mildly flirtatious—smile, and Renald buried his notice of it in the dainty china cup.

"And the Comanche chief?" said Mrs. Hermann. "The one who went looking? I read that he is your nephew, Mr. Renald."

His creased brow expressed his irritation. "We don't get to choose our relatives, now do we?" Convinced of his nephew's double dealing, he added, "What we let those Indians get away with—allowing them back on the reservation like nothing happened, rather than hanging them as horse thieves and murderers. Why, we even give 'em passes to hunt on their old hunting grounds!" He lowered his voice, conscious of a customer or two attempting to listen in from the bar counter. "Anyway, here's where the story turns in your favor, Mrs. Hermann."

"In my favor, Mr. Renald?" She sat up in her chair. "How could it?"

"Karl told us he'd traded with a Comanche camp about a half-day's ride north of the supply point, at Rich Lake," he said. "When I heard this, I thought we might even find the breakouts there, or at least learn where they went. Well, while I was still en route to the supply depot—having delivered the water—Trooper Tyler went ahead and found the camp Karl spoke of. No breakout party, but from his vantage point he thought he saw a black girl among the Indians."

"A black girl?" Mrs. Hermann's voice throbbed. "Emma Neely?"

Renald cast a sidelong glare at an eavesdropping customer, then continued, "By the time Tyler got back to the depot, I was packing up to return with additional water. He took charge of the water detail instead, and I rode north for the girl. I confess I looked for her *last,* but just think—that colored troop never got orders to look for her at all."

As if Emma Neely were her own child, Mrs. Hermann began wiping away tears. "Tell me you found her …"

"I didn't," he said. "But here's what did happen."

He drained his cup. "I rode straight into the small Quahada camp. Just eight or nine lodges and a store of twenty or so horses, which frankly looked better fed than their owners. I was quickly recognized by an old headman, and I knew then I wasn't risking my life. Normally, if the reception is warm, I'm invited to dine and smoke with the chief, and normally I accept and show respect before making any request. But seeing that the fighting men were absent—they'd run off with the breakouts, you see—I simply dismounted and demanded the girl as if it was known she was there. Well, the old man told me they had, in fact, adopted a black girl some moons ago. They hadn't stolen her, he said—a young Apache warrior had done that. His raiding party had come up short and he couldn't return without something of value for his chief—so he snatched her from Chadbourne and traded her for a horse." Renald paused. "He was a white warrior, ma'am."

"*Mein Gott,*" Trude gasped, raising her hands to her face. "*Mein Sohn,* three times a murderer, you say—and a robber of *Kinder.*"

Renald raised a hand. "Remember, I said this is where the story turns in your favor, ma'am. Something to make you proud." He let her collect herself before he continued. "The girl," he said, "had been placed in the care of a squaw who'd lost her husband and sons to war, the chief told me. Lest I disbelieve him, he showed me to her lonely wickiup. There I found her in mourning—by no means a young squaw at that. Rocking back and forth, she chanted through her sobs, clutching a child's white nightdress."

"But what happened to the little one? To poor Emma?"

"According to the chief, the previous night that very same white warrior returned to reclaim her—and nobody was present to oppose him."

Her elevated voice registered her alarm. "And for what did he want her?"

"I reckon Karl came to the conclusion that a hero of old doesn't steal another man's child, sure not the child of a hero who helped save his brother."

Mrs. Hermann's eyes shone with a fresh varnish of tears.

With that, Renald dug into his breast pocket and withdrew a light blue, onion-skin envelope. He opened it, unfolding a piece of stationery. "If you please, this here letter was awaiting my return yesterday from Fort McKavett. It's signed 'Mrs. Florence Neely, Old Fort Chadbourne,' and it reads like it was written on her behalf. *For* her, I mean. Most of the black folk out here were slaves once, the troopers … their wives. Didn't get much schooling, if any."

He commenced reading aloud the story of a white Indian returning the Neelys' missing daughter in good health and in native garb. " 'Before the brave rode back toward the setting sun,' she writes, 'my husband inquired of him the reason for returning our dear Emma. The youth seemed to understand the question but could not reply, having lost the ability to speak our language. After several halting attempts, he simply answered with your name, sir, so we deduced that you had a role in her rescue. For this, we sincerely …' and so on."

Renald folded the letter, then transferred the envelope into Trude Hermann's hand. "In this," he whispered, "Karl has come as close to you as he could."

A quiet moment passed. "Is there no hope he will come home?" she asked.

Struggling for an answer, Renald replied, "With us, Karl was never more than a boy … but as Endah he became a man. A boy leaves home to become one." This simple explanation might convince Mrs. Hermann, and Renald couldn't think of anything better.

Trude Hermann rested her gaze thoughtfully on the envelope in her hand, all but weightless and yet of monumental import. Gathering her breath, she carefully placed it aside on the tablecloth. Then, surprising even himself, Renald reached across the table and took her hands in his. His blush mirroring her own, he said with conviction, "Now, Trude, about you and Freddie …"

Acknowledgments

This novel starts with an epigraph that may have taken some readers by surprise. For what relevant thoughts could Edgar Rice Burroughs' *Tarzan of the Apes* possibly offer a novel about the American frontier? The Prologue, I think, answers the question.

The 19th century saw an explosion in literature of fantastical adventures—known as "science fiction" today—from visionaries such as Jules Verne and H.G. Wells. Verne called his stories "voyages extraordinaires." In the early 20th century, Burroughs followed spectacularly on their heels with his "scientific romances" of this world and others.

While certainly less fantasy-driven than any works produced by those authors, in tone and spirit *The Unredeemed* owes more to Burroughs' *Tarzan of the Apes* than to any story of the American frontier except, perhaps, Herman Lehmann's own nonfiction account. But the Tarzan of books was by no means that character's sole influence on the tale told here. Fans of the two best Tarzan films, 1959's *Tarzan's Greatest Adventure* and 1960's *Tarzan the Magnificent,* will recognize something of the longbow-wielding Gordon Scott as Tarzan in the white

Apache, Endah. Movie buffs may also recognize a nod to *She Wore a Yellow Ribbon* in Scott Renald's soliloquy at his late wife's headstone.

As ever, I am grateful to my long-ago editorial colleague at *The Prague Revue,* David Speranza, for his early review of the manuscript. Gerlinde Dringenberg, another friend from Prague, corrected the German language in the text, while literary translator and friend Alicia Frieyro improved the Spanish. Additionally, the crime novelist Diane Piron-Gelman, my editor on this novel's predecessor, *Comanche Captive*, returned to Indian country with me to give the book a final polish. I would also like to acknowledge the generous investment Tom Mayer has made in Broken Arrow Press, and Alan Long for his exceptional administrative help Stateside. My terrifically supportive parents, too, warrant mention. More than any mentor, my mother, Wallys Conhaim, once a pioneering journalist in "new information technologies," taught me how to write and, more importantly, how not to write; meantime my history-devoted father, Roger, unveiled the American West with real excitement and dedication during numerous camping and hiking trips in my youth.

Finally, a special appreciation to Dennis Gormley, a retired New Jersey police detective and fan of *Comanche Captive*, who has sent boxes of western novels and histories to my residences in Israel and Minnesota. His correspondences all close with a message that bears repeating at the end of this novel: "Cherish your family every day."

Afterword

The Buffalo Soldier Tragedy of 1877 is one of the Old West's most harrowing chapters, and yet we hardly remember it. To be sure, other setbacks for the U.S. Cavalry were costlier in lives, making The Little Big Horn and Fetterman massacres more historically memorable. But the crisis that befell 10th Troop was unusual for several reasons: in full, it played out over eleven days, was complicated by a mixed racial dynamic, and included the involvement of the last great Comanche headman, Quanah Parker.

The half-white Parker inspired the character of Talking Moon in this novel's predecessor, *Comanche Captive*, and by continuing Talking Moon's story here while remaining consistent with Quanah Parker's own career arc,[2] I was able

---

[2] Quanah Parker's story never ceases to amaze. From war leader to successful rancher to President Theodore Roosevelt's hunting partner to founder of the peyote-driven Native American Church Movement, his story is one of singular accomplishment and novelty. Talking Moon's business relationship with Cole Hawker is loosely based on Parker's with rancher Burk Burnett.

to reexamine Parker's debated connection to the Buffalo Soldier Tragedy.

To the reader, my merging of the lost cavalry expedition with Scott Renald's quest for the white warrior might seem a fanciful exercise. In actual fact, there was a connection between the troop tragedy and a missing white boy. As the Author's Note indicates, Endah/Karl is based partly on Herman Lehmann, a white Indian who was among the Comanche holdouts found and brought in by Quanah Parker that very year of 1877.

A white Indian? The term is intended to define Endah culturally and ironically against the white man who has come to "redeem" him. In this sense, "Indian" describes his citizenship—i.e., belonging to an American Indian nation—just as my immigrant grandparents belonged to the United States of America: László and Lea's accents may have made them different from the norm, but they were indisputable members of their adoptive nation.

With regard to Emma Neely's difficult journey, though black children became Indian captives alongside white children in the American West, I have yet to find any reference to an organized search for an abducted African-American child. If a stolen black girl did not spur the U.S. Cavalry or the Texas Rangers—or even a posse—into action, then what incentive existed for her abductors to hold her for trade? Unlikely to be sought after, she was adopted.[3]

---

[3] Or enslaved. Slavery among the tribes of the Southwest—which took slaves of each other—was commonly a step toward becoming a member of the tribe, reconstituting the fighting force, etc. Except in trade, in those parts the slave was not treated as chattel for very long. Black slaves were greatly more numerous among the so-called "Five Civilized Tribes" of the Southeastern United States, which practiced plantation-style slavery and accepted and assimilated black runaway slaves. Thousands of black

Southern Cheyenne family, 1886

Perhaps the most notable African Americans to be rescued from Indian captivity were the wife and children of Britt Johnson. In 1864, this Texas foreman (possibly a slave at the time) lost a son in the Elm Creek Raid, and—the story goes—searched high and low among the Comanche and Kiowa for his surviving family members, eventually rescuing them from the Kiowa. If true, even in part, Johnson's legendary exploits were done alone, reinforcing

---

slaves migrated with the Cherokee, Chickasaw, Choctaw, Creek, and the Seminole to Indian Territory in the 1830s and '40s—the so-called "Trail of Tears." In 1850, Frederick Douglass wrote, "A slave among wild Indians is almost as free as his owner. The slave finds more of the milk of human kindness in the bosom of the savage Indian, than in the heart of his Christian master." By 1860, it is estimated that the Cherokee alone possessed around 4,000 black slaves.

my suspicion that organized recovery efforts were reserved only for white people.[4]

This novel hints at homosexuality in Native American culture. Missionaries of the time—though their criteria and therefore their judgment might be questioned—reported witnessing overt male homosexuality in tribe after tribe, band after band. According to Sabine Lang and Thomas Jacobs (*Two-Spirit People: Native American Gender Identity, Sexuality, and Spirituality,* University of Illinois Press, 1997), "two-spirits" were found among Mohave medicine men, and in the Lipan, Mescalero, and Chiricahua bands of the Apache where alternative gender identities were accepted.[5]

While much of the novel's historical detail is trustworthy, ample literary license has been exercised as well. To start with some examples that a West Texan might spot, herein the town of Ben Ficklin sits on the *west* bank of the South Concho River, and Fort Concho is surrounded by a stockade that never existed.

---

[4] Some credit the Comanche chief Asa-Havey with the Johnson family's return as a peace gesture. There is little more than oral history to reference, though the occurrence of the Elm Creek Raid, in which a total of seven captives were taken, including the Johnsons, is not disputed. Many such raids would immediately follow, according to "Texas Beyond History," a virtual museum of the University of Texas at Austin. It reports, "… 163 settlers killed by Indians, 24 wounded, and 43 carried away from the summer of 1865 through the summer of 1867."

[5] The reader is also referred to "Lesbians in Native American Culture" by Paula Gunn Allen, *The Sacred Hoop,* Beacon Press, second edition, 1992, regarding how female homosexuality may have fit into tribal life. The term "two-spirit" to describe pan-Indian third gender roles, however, does not appear in her essay, as it was not widely used until a decade after initial publication in 1981. Part Laguna and Sioux, Gunn Allen interestingly rejected the term "Native American" as a product of the academy, preferring "American Indian."

Renamed sites on the map in Part IV might raise some eyebrows too. In addition, De B. Randolph Keim's "Sheridan's Views on the Indian Question" appeared in Washington D.C.'s *Evening Star,* whereas the text implies it was a printed book. Finally, the term "teenager" did not come into use until the 1940s.

Regarding the Native American peoples described herein, while I have taken pains to get many historical and cultural details right, I'm elsewhere guilty of taking liberties and painting with a broad brush. A prime example is Chivatá's use of the modern term "two-spirit" (see footnote #5 above).

Making more substantial appearances in *The Unredeemed* than in its predecessor *Comanche Captive* are Captain Norton and Sergeant Chance. Their names recall, respectively, Cpt. Nicholas Nolan, who—true history be told—survived the horror and avoided official rebuke,[6] and Sgt. Emanuel Stance, who was awarded the Medal of Honor for rescuing Herman Lehmann's younger brother, Willie, shortly after their abduction by the Apache. Trooper Tyler, who received the barest mention in this novel's predecessor, is an intended homage to Ben Johnson's Sgt. Tyree in the inspiring John Ford cavalry pictures *She Wore a Yellow Ribbon* (1949) and *Rio Grande* (1950).

As for commissioned officers, specifically the rank of lieutenant, the narrative offers three explanations for why no one in the temporary command chain exists between Sgt. Chance

---

[6] Hence the name change. Sadly, whereas Nicholas Nolan avoided any consequences at all, four black troopers serving under him were dishonorably discharged and imprisoned despite the highly debatable circumstances of their "desertion." Also worth noting here is that the story of Ophelia Wheatman, told early in the book, bears substantial resemblance to the true life story of Indian captive Olive Oatman, but, according to the author's conscience, is divergent enough to warrant the amended name.

and Cpt. Norton: The escort required to deliver Lt. Col. Davidson to Fort Custer, family leave, and historical troop reassignments to the Mexican border. These allowed me to develop Chance's relationship with Norton and Davidson. In actual fact, a Lieutenant Charles Cooper played a major role in events as Nolan's immediate subordinate.

Regarding our unreliable Indian guide, Chivatá, aficionados of the period will recognize in her a striking resemblance to the beautiful Chiricahua rebel, Lozen. Yet, by extending Chivatá's quest with Renald to include the Buffalo Soldier Tragedy, I necessarily melded her already enigmatic person with an additional historical figure, that of José Piedad Tafoya, the infamous "Prince of the Comancheros," who is thought by some to have struck a deal with Quanah Parker to lead the troop into nowhere. The deal purportedly involved a portion of the renegades' plunder.[7]

A Hollywood climax might have seen Chivatá declaring vengeance hers for Norton's massacre of the Northern People. I preferred a more ambiguous one that, while diverging from

---

[7] An alternative interpretation, and one posited by Paul H. Carlson in his straightforwardly titled *The Buffalo Soldier Tragedy of 1877* (Texas A&M University Press, 2003), sees Parker misleading Tafoya as payback. For what? In Carlson's version, in 1874 Tafoya gives up the location of the Comanche holdouts and their allies, resulting in the army's overwhelming success in the Battle of Palo Duro Canyon. Interestingly, like Carlson's contradictory documentation of Tafoya's efforts to *save* the troop (referring to Tafoya as "the honest, loyal, and gallant company guide"), the historian paints a more favorable picture than others have of Nolan's true First Sergeant, William Umbles. Later courtmartialed, dishonorably discharged, and sentenced to imprisonment at Leavenworth for desertion, Umbles reportedly allowed the men to drink alcohol before the expedition got underway—a piece of the story that Carlson curiously omits rather than refutes.

the historical record, remains consistent with the tragedy's enduring mystery. Hence both fiction and fact deliver the same lasting question. Was this merely a mishandled expedition, or was 10th Troop's horror a native people's victory in their life-or-death struggle?

About the Author

Born in Minneapolis in 1968, D. László Conhaim's first professional writing credit was a two-part 1986 interview in Los Angeles and Tokyo with Japanese film legend Toshiro Mifune for Minnesota weekly *City Pages*. In 1995, Conhaim co-founded *The Prague Revue*, the longest-running literary journal to serve the community of international writers in Prague. For *TPR*, he wrote a fictional remembrance of Miguel de Unamuno, "Feeling into Don Miguel," which Gore Vidal "read with delight" and Alexander Zaitchik (*Rolling Stone*, *The Nation*) called "masterful" in *Think Magazine*. In 1999, TPR Books published his corresponding novel *Autumn Serenade*. In 2017, Cengage/Five Star released *Comanche Captive* in hardback, the first installment of a Western trilogy whose final installment, *All Man's Land*, was published to acclaim in 2019 by Broken Arrow Press, winning the Will Rogers Medallion "Maverick" Award and placing Finalist Best Novel in the Western Writers of America Spur Awards. Chronologically, *The Unredeemed* (Broken Arrow Press, 2021) falls between those two titles, completing the cycle. Whereas, *Comanche Captive* is dedicated to Conhaim's son, Ziv, *The Unredeemed* is dedicated to Ziv's younger sister Shir. The Conhaims live in Israel.

Made in the USA
Coppell, TX
09 February 2022

73294364R00146